⏥DAN

A Shot at Democracy

A Kirsten Stewart Thriller

First edition

ISBN: 978-1-914073-43-4

This book was professionally typeset on Reedsy. Find out more at reedsy.com

The whole problem with the world is that fools and fanatics are always so certain of themselves, and wiser people so full of doubts.

BERTRAND RUSSELL

Contents

Foreword

This story is set in the north of Scotland based around occurrences in Inverness. Although incorporating known cities, towns and villages, note that all events, persons, structures and specific places are fictional and not to be confused with actual buildings and structures which have been used as an inspirational canvas to tell a completely fictional story.

Acknowledgement

To Susan, Jean and Rosemary for your work in bringing this novel to completion, your time and effort is deeply appreciated.

Novels by G R Jordan

The Highlands and Islands Detective series (Crime)

1. Water's Edge
2. The Bothy
3. The Horror Weekend
4. The Small Ferry
5. Dead at Third Man
6. The Pirate Club
7. A Personal Agenda
8. A Just Punishment
9. The Numerous Deaths of Santa Claus
10. Our Gated Community
11. The Satchel
12. Culhwch Alpha
13. Fair Market Value

Kirsten Stewart Thrillers (Thriller)

1. A Shot at Democracy
2. The Hunted Child

The Contessa Munroe Mysteries (Cozy Mystery)

1. Corpse Reviver
2. Frostbite
3. Cobra's Fang

The Patrick Smythe Series (Crime)

1. The Disappearance of Russell Hadleigh
2. The Graves of Calgary Bay
3. The Fairy Pools Gathering

Austerley & Kirkgordon Series (Fantasy)

1. Crescendo!
2. The Darkness at Dillingham
3. Dagon's Revenge
4. Ship of Doom

Supernatural and Elder Threat Assessment Agency (SETAA) Series (Fantasy)

1. Scarlett O'Meara: Beastmaster

Island Adventures Series (Cosy Fantasy Adventure)

1. Surface Tensions

Dark Wen Series (Horror Fantasy)

Chapter 1

'That's the cash for Glasgow. Client was happy. Good job—neat and tidy. Police are still chasing around with no idea who they are after. They're claiming gang warfare. He set the cat right amongst the pigeons.'

'Completed as asked, no questions. Give us the cash?'

'But, of course, here you go.'

From her position just outside the door, Kirsten Stewart heard what sounded like a duffel bag being thrown at the request of the cash. Her heart was pounding for they were coming to it, the moment when after a month's work, she would bring her first major catch in her career working with the secret services.

They had been operating a hitman in Glasgow, allegedly taking from both sides whatever job came along, and as her boss said, stirring things up into a gang war. None of it was the hitman's fault. Whoever was setting him up was definitely playing both sides, and reaping a lot of cash in the process.

'It's all there then,' said the first speaker's voice. This was the fixer— Alastair Carlton—who'd set up the jobs.

'Yes, it's all there. Don't talk to me. Just ring the number. Then we'll meet; you know where.' The abrupt answer was

1

given by James Gunn, a man with an apt surname, for he was a hired gun, a hitman by profession. He had made a name for himself maybe ten years ago, and now had come back out of retirement. Maybe the money had run dry. Who knew? He was causing such a commotion in the city of Glasgow, that extra help had been sought from the UK's secret services. Newly qualified Kirsten Stewart had been an integral part of the team who were now about to bring both men to justice.

The location for this meeting was a small ruin just outside Inverness despite the hour being two o'clock in the morning. Stewart could see just a little daylight. That was because the sun never really went down here in the summer. Yes, it maybe peeked behind the sofa for a while, but then it came back up, so there was only ever a twilight, never a full darkness. Not that the night was particularly warm, and a light drizzle was falling outside.

Stewart's hand was positioned at her holster, ready to draw her weapon, but she knew how dangerous the two men inside were. There would be no questions, no wonder that she was there. Instead, if they knew she was there, a blast of gunfire would follow. Her superior had warned her about this. Although she regretted using weapons, she had taken it onboard and was ready to use whatever measures were necessary if this operation should go wrong.

It all seemed a far cry from the days of working with Macleod. There was a deep fondness for her former mentor and for the man who had pushed her—or as he put it, given his blessing—to move from the police force into the more shadowy side of crime-fighting. In her time on the murder squad, she'd seen plenty of bodies and a myriad of people with reasons to kill, but now she was doing things less in the open. Covert surveillance for the main, gathering intelligence, understanding what the situation was, and then moving in for a swift operation that would grab these two particular snakes they were after.

Kirsten could hear the duffel bag being pulled across again as if someone was about to leave, but then she heard a brief cough.

'Before you go, how did the other one go?' It was the voice of Alastair Carlton, and it seemed that another job had been opened up for James Gunn.

'Not for me. I came back into this to get a bit of cash, not to go off my ruddy head.'

'What do you mean?'

'We don't talk about it, do we?' said Gunn. 'What are the rules? You set up the job. I do it or I don't; you don't ask about it.'

'I'll ask about it if I want. Listen, Jimmy. I thought this was a good source, lucrative too. I want to know why not. You're not the only one who puts his arse on the line. I have to work out a cover, go and see these people, talk, lose tails, make sure I'm not seen. I don't get to pull a gun when it all goes wrong.'

'You don't need to tell me the business,' Gunn retorted. 'I told you. It was too much.'

'You've just taken out some of the top people in Glasgow. What's too much?'

'Wrong side of the fence. Government, that side, not my sort of thing.'

'They never said anything about government. Are you sure?'

'Well, that's what I reckon, government or somebody in the headlines. Maybe that woman off TV. Who knows? Somebody on that level though. Too much exposure. Not like putting down a couple of criminals. Who really gives a damn about them? They'd be after you for this one. After me too, and I don't need that sort of heat.'

'They told you that, did they? Did you get the target?'

'Don't be stupid,' said Gunn. 'Of course, I didn't get the target. The last thing I would want if I'm not getting paid to do it. I just told them, no. Firm and fair, and no questions asked.'

'They let you walk? There wasn't any comeback?'

'Well, I'm here, aren't I? The sort of money they were talking and the type of target they were hinting at, if they thought there would be trouble, if they thought I could spill anything, I wouldn't be here.'

Kirsten could hear one of the men begin to move off and her hand reached for her weapon gripping it tightly.

'I guess that's it then,' said Gunn. 'You know the name. You know the number. Next time you've got something. But something with a little less heat then, obviously. Just something, anything, but not that hot. I'm here to earn my pension, not end up back in jail.'

Stewart could hear Gunn begin to move and she placed her weapon in front of her, waiting for the man to walk through the door. With her free hand, she tapped the button on her signaller, a small device kept in her pocket. By double-clicking, it let the rest of the team know that they were about to move in. She would have spoken through her comm link, but she felt she was too close, and might be overheard.

The building was located off the main road but hidden behind a number of bushes, which meant that the darkness was thick. Although the sky was far from black, with streaks of morning light beginning to ignite the interior of the room, it was hard to see. Stewart was all attention, her ears listening to the footsteps that were coming closer to her. In front of her, she saw a large man of at least six foot two stepping forward. He wore a black jacket, black trousers, and a happy grin. Over his shoulder was a duffel bag, possibly green, but hard to see in the light. Stewart gently pressed her weapon into the man's neck.

'Don't move. Slowly put the bag down. Keep your hands out so I can see them at all times.'

Stewart could hear movement in the rest of the house and knew the team was moving in to pick up Alastair Carlton. There was a brief cry from the man. After all the effort and drama of finding the pair, the pick-up was simple, smooth, and effective. A few minutes later, Stewart was watching as two of her colleagues escorted James Gunn into the rear of a car, and he was driven off at speed. Alastair Carlton followed in a different car. Stewart was left with some communication officers and her boss.

Unlike Stewart, her boss was dressed in a tight but long skirt with a sharp jacket over the top. She had tights on too, down to where her legs should have ended in a trim pair of heels. Instead, Stewart could see walking boots. The ground around the house was uneven, and anyone in heels would have fallen over.

Stewart had been prepared, and had come in her black jeans, her leather jacket, and black boots. She thought that the dark purple hair that she now sported might match neatly with the jacket. For once, Kirsten felt she had achieved what her previous boss, Hope McGrath, seemed to do without trying: to look like a professional, smart, and possibly even sexy officer. Unlike the six-foot McGrath, Stewart was smaller, a little thicker set, and not so self-assured. But she packed a punch, something they had found out at the training college during hand-to-hand combat exercises. She had disarmed and disabled male colleague after male colleague.

'Good work tonight, Stewart, but back to the safe house. We'll take them and get them debriefed so I want to see you there in about two hours' time. Let everybody get wrapped up here first before we start doing the interviews.'

'Do you mind if I take a detour?'

'Your brother again, is it?'

'Yes, boss, my brother.' Kirsten Stewart's brother resided in a home for those who were mentally challenged. In his particular case, having a form of dementia, he struggled to remember from day to day people who have been in his life. Kirsten had struggled to see him, but on the few days when she had, and he was up and about, it nearly broke her heart when he didn't even recognize her.

Her brother spoke of a man that came to see him, older, and who he reckoned was possibly his dad. It was Kirsten's old boss, Macleod. He knew Kirsten couldn't always get to the home, couldn't always see her brother, and he'd been dropping in to make sure everything was all right. Because of this, Kirsten had taken to dropping in at night when the people in the home would let her watch her brother as he slept.

'Just make sure you're there when we start the interviews,' said her boss. 'By the way, did you clock it?'

'Yes, I clocked it.'

'Do you believe it?' asked Stewart's boss. Kirsten turned and looked at the woman. Anna Hunt was often a difficult woman to read. She had the ability to deliver every sentence with the same face. She never looked sad. She never looked happy. She never looked anything. A contrast to Stewart, who could go through a range of emotions. The woman was wiry but looked thin and tall when standing beside Stewart.

'Do you think there's something in it?' asked Stewart.

'One can't tell if there's anything in it. Somebody was certainly made an offer for something. My money says these guys won't talk, but we'll see. I thought this would close this case,' said Anna. 'I thought that we would be done, possibly heading back towards Glasgow, but I think I might have to leave you in a field office up here. We'll see once we get to talk to these guys. But you know, gunmen being gunmen, I'm not sure they'll say much. I'll see you back at the safe house. I hope your brother's okay.'

'My brother's dead to the world, at least dead to my world,' said Kirsten. She realized there was a melancholy about her these days. When she had worked with Macleod, she was always on the go, always ready, but with her brother disappearing from her life but yet still being alive, she felt like she should grieve. *But how could she? How do you grieve over somebody who's still alive?*

Taking leave of her boss, Stewart climbed inside her car. It was over ten years old, banged up and beaten, but was a solid performer as she drove towards the centre of Inverness. The night-duty nurse at the home recognized her in the front porch, opened the door, and simply gave her a wave as Kirsten walked in. Kirsten raised her hand in acknowledgement, but there was no smile. She made her way along the corridors until she came to a room with a small white plaque showing a one and a seven.

Slowly, she opened the door, hearing the light snores that were coming from inside. The home itself was cheery enough, but at night the dim lights provided an eerie mood. Inside her brother's room, everything was dark. The curtains were thick set, and despite the flowery pattern, she felt the room to be extremely basic. There was a small desk beside the bed and Kirsten saw a photograph of herself and another of her parents.

The nurse had told Kirsten that every time her brother got up in the morning, he asked who these people were. Kirsten thought she should label them, a big hand pointing to her saying, 'Kirsten', but they'd advised against it. Better to accept what was then try and force her brother back to see a person he had left some time ago.

Kirsten stood in the dark watching the snoring figure in the bed. Her brother always lay on his back, face up to the ceiling, eyes shut tight, his mouth blowing open like a whale's blowhole.

She saw his chest rise and fall. Part of her wondered would it be better if it didn't do that but simply stopped, so he could go on to whatever lay beyond, and she could go on with her life. A tear ran down her face, and she reached up to wipe it away. Yes, it had been good to be up in Inverness, good to be back up the road to stop in and see him every night, but she couldn't do this forever. Her heart wouldn't allow her to.

Chapter 2

Stewart parked her black Corsa out on the street in the old town of Inverness. She walked along the dimly lit pavement looking up at a terrace row that had been there for years until she came to the front door of an office for Trans-Nation. There was flaking paint on the door and the whole building looked remarkably drab. Taking out her key, she opened the front lock, pushed the door open, and stepped inside. Once she had closed the door, Kirsten paused for a moment to listen. There were voices upstairs. She walked through the porch and rapped the door on her left-hand side before making her way into the front room of the ground floor. In the darkness behind a table was a man looking at his phone. The brightness of the screen lit up the man's face showing he hadn't shaved in three or four days, but he had a smile and a nod for her.

'All right, Angel.'

She hated the codename, and it was the man across from her that dreamt it up. Stewart thought that Justin Chivers was something of a recluse. He certainly didn't look like an operative of the secret services. He was overweight by some amount and in truth, got out of breath when he climbed the stairs inside the building, but the man's mind was sharp and he certainly knew how to work a computer. Stewart was no mug in that department but even she was impressed with what the man could come up with. What she wasn't impressed with was the way his eyes always scanned her. She'd mentioned it once to her boss, but Anna Hunt had told her that the man was too valuable to replace.

'Yes, he's a bit of a dirty boy,' Anna had said, 'but if it gets too much, just give him a slap; you have my permission. As long as he's functioning afterwards.'

'That's me checking in, Chivers. I'll be upstairs.' Kirsten turned on her heel. It felt like eyes were watching her as she left the room. Kirsten had not given him a slap yet because she realized it wouldn't be a simple slap, it would be a full-on punch and the man might not function afterwards. Luckily, she didn't see him every day since she worked out in the field more than the office. Still, his behaviour would need to be tamed. If it got any worse, it would be.

Climbing stairs that were carpeted in a 1970s pattern of rather depressing browns and greys, Stewart made her way past another man who stood on the small landing of the first floor. He was dressed in a neat suit and she recognized him as Anna Hunt's bodyguard. Of course, he wasn't given that title, but effectively that was who he was. He went everywhere with her unless, of course, things were so important that his presence would pose a risk. The general dogsbody, that's how Anna would put it. Not that clever either. Yet Kirsten found Richard Lafferty to be charming and polite in all things.

'She's waiting for you, Kirsten,' said Richard with a smile. 'I think she's pretty pleased with you as well. Nice one tonight.'

Kirsten forced a smile back. After seeing her brother, she

was feeling pretty down. Still, she had done a good job. Even Macleod would have had to say so. She really needed to stop doing this, referring everything back to her previous boss. Macleod, McGrath, and even Ross had played a vital part in her life and career, but now she had to go and work more in the dark. Anna Hunt wasn't like Macleod. You received instructions, but you also got a lot of vagueness. You were expected to make your own judgments at times and not refer everything back. Then again, it was a slightly different role she was undertaking.

Stewart made her way across the first floor, opening a door at the far end. In the room beyond was a carpeted floor, a table, and four plastic chairs. Sitting in two of the plastic chairs were the apprehended men, hands tied up behind their backs. The other chair was empty, and standing behind it was Anna Hunt. She didn't look at Stewart as she entered but simply raised her nose to the air.

'Right, let's begin.'

Stewart was unsure as to whether or not she should sit down. Her boss often liked to take the lead in interviews so Stewart made her way to the corner of the room, leaning and lifting one foot up off the floor tucking it behind her other leg.

'Right, gentlemen. I don't need to know what went down in Glasgow because we *know* what went down in Glasgow. We've got enough to throw it at you, and that side's getting handed over. Before you leave this room, you're going to tell me what that other conversation was about.'

'What conversation?' asked Alastair Carlton. He was sitting back in his chair quite relaxed with a vague smile on his face. Kirsten found his act of nonchalance impressive, considering the fact that he was now bang to rights and would end up going to prison. Carlton was only the middleman and maybe he reckoned prison would be no threat. He was known for not opening his mouth and had spent time there before, albeit a two-year sentence.

'The little matter that you and James were discussing. The other job, the one James didn't take.'

Stewart saw Gunn looking across at Carlton, his eyes full of anger, 'I told you, we don't talk about things. Never, but you did. And now look at us.'

'Yes. What do you care? You're going to prison for a while,' said Carlton, 'just keep your mouth shut.'

'That's the problem, isn't it?' said Gunn, 'It doesn't matter if you keep your mouth shut or not. Now, these people are starting to put their nose in. They think you've spoken. You arsehole, Carlton. You utter arsehole, you had to bring that up.'

'If you let me know what's going on, I can always get you some protection. Put you away into the scheme.'

Kirsten Stewart watched Anna Hunt as she made the offer. Stewart was unsure whether it was sincere or not. Of course, she had heard it said that even the scheme couldn't keep you clear of certain people. And the pair were so afraid that James Gunn had not taken the job from these people. Maybe they were the sort the scheme wouldn't work for.

'I am not saying anything,' said Gunn. 'I'll go in and I'll do my rap. They might come for me but you know what? I haven't spoken. I'm no grass. No, they'll not come for me, more like Carlton. Yes, somebody will come for you, Carlton.'

Stewart watched Carlton's face as the man seemed to grow more and more anxious. 'What about you, Mr. Carlton?' said Anna. 'Looks like you could do with protection. I can certainly keep you away from this guy.'

'Nobody keeps you away from them.'

'Who's them?' said Stewart. 'Who is them?'

'Who's the target?' asked Anna. 'You said government.'

'If you'd been listening,' said Gunn, 'I said something like government, popstar, something hot. Something beyond everybody else. One you don't go after because of the media interest. One that would have you running off to Mexico for the rest of your life. Hell, I do like this country. I was born and raised in Scotland and I'll damn well stay here even if it's behind the bars of one of her majesty's prisons. I'm not dumb enough to take on a job like that.'

'Who offered the job?' queried Anna.

'Now I wouldn't know that, would I?' said Gunn. 'You know how this works. I have a contact, I meet, I get told a poor picture of what's occurring. I stopped him. I stopped him the moment he talked about a high profile public figure. That's what he said. Those four words. High profile public figure. What the hell was that? I was in this for my pension. I was in this to get some cash and get the damn well out. Spend six months in Glasgow, six months out somewhere sunny. Some woman on my arm and the money to see my days through. That's all I wanted. That's all they said. High profile public figure.'

'Who said?' Stewart looked at her boss. The line of questioning wasn't going to work.

'Where did they say it?' asked Stewart. 'Where did you meet?'

Gunn looked at her and smiled. 'You haven't been in this game long, love, have you? If we were in America, I'd probably be pooing my pants because they'd been sending me somewhere, wouldn't they? To a place where they beat you and whatever else. That's what they do. Especially if they thought the threat was high. That's what all those programs say, isn't it?'

'If you know something, they'll not leave you alone here either,' said Anna. 'We have ways and means.'

'Then use your ways and your means if you want. As for me, I need a piss.'

'You'll sit there. I don't care if you piss your pants,' said Anna. 'I don't care until you tell me something about the person who gave you that description. As for you, Mr. Carlton, I want to know what the hell's going on. I want to know where your contact came from.'

'Deposit box. Dropped in. People know that's how you contact me. Didn't say much. Said I had a job and requested James. That's it. I didn't know about the high public profile. If I did, I'd been telling them what sort of money it was. I'd have told James beforehand and he wouldn't have rejected the job. That's how it works. That's the point of me. I'm meant to be there to work out how you do things if this was high profile.'

'Oh, gentlemen, is that all you've really given me?' With that, Anna Hunt turned on her heel, opened the door of the room, and waved Richard Lafferty in. 'Babysit this lot, Rick. The only thing they get is a coffee, no food. Don't let them sleep. If Mr. Gunn wants the toilet, tell him he can piss his pants because piss is what he's given me.'

Kirsten Stewart left the room with her boss, amazed as ever about how such a classy-dressed woman could be so vulgar. It wasn't in Kirsten's nature. Anna saw this as a fault. She'd always told Kirsten she needed to handle people, treat them like they should be treated. These lowlifes should be handled as such. Of course, she was well aware of human rights. Sure, you had to play on the edge of the lines but for Stewart felt like she always played them on the wrong side.

'What do you make of that?' asked Hunt as she opened the door to another small room. Inside there was a desk with a computer and a leather chair that Hunt flopped into. This was Kirsten's office, but her boss let her know that when she was here, Anna Hunt had full run.

'I doubt we'll get anything from them.'

'I doubt it too,' said Anna, 'but it's intriguing. I don't think this is a wild goose chase; certainly don't believe this is nothing. Let's run it through the mill because Carlton brought it up. Yes, Carlton was interested enough to ask. Gunn said to him, "This isn't for him. It's not what we do." Therefore, there must have been something in their message to Carlton. Tell me, Stewart, where do we go next? If we're not getting anything out of these two, what do I do with this information?'

Stewart hated this. Macleod would have just said to you, 'Have you got any thoughts?' but not this woman. Anna Hunt always had to put everything down like a test. 'We round up well-known associates, people who would contact him. There must be a chain, a link of some sort.'

'Smart thinking,' said Anna. 'If you're going to ask somebody to do this, you're going to expect him to take it on. I think somebody might have screwed up laying down contracts. Often more than one middle-man is used. I think that's where we need to go. I can chase the tail from the office, put feelers out and see what's going on. See if there's any chatter, anything big that only other departments know about. I want you to trace Carlton's contacts for me. Have a look, see if anybody seems a little bit wary, behaving abnormally. Shake the tree and see what falls, Kirsten. You understand?'

'Perfectly.'

'As for the rest of us, I'm taking this lot back to Glasgow so the office goes dead except for yourself as of today. Let me know how you get on if anything comes out of it. I'm back in Glasgow, possibly elsewhere.'

Well, tonight was something, Kirsten thought. She enjoyed being part of a team when she was in the murder squad, but it was different running the secret services. There was an air of distrust while checking everyone all the time. She didn't consider herself a spy, simply a police officer, a detective working in slightly greyer areas, a necessary evil because of the things that were done out in the world. Part of her missed the team, missed having someone like Macleod or even Hope McGrath to lean on, to ask questions of. Here you were expected to deduce on your own and if you got it wrong, you would fall, not the boss.

Kirsten watched Anna Hunt rise from her chair and make her way across to the door of the room. Jumping into the warm seat, Kirsten took her glasses off the desk, and placed them on her nose before taking them off quickly again. She had contacts on because it gave her a different appearance. It was why she changed her hair colour too, and would change it more again. But she found it hard to get rid of that old routine, where she used to pop the glasses on her nose and push them up.

'That's a tell-tale you need to cut out,' said Anna. 'Keep it sharp.' The woman closed the door hard behind her and Stewart realized that the pep talk was over, if you could call it that. A glance at her watch showed 4:00 a.m. *Okay, Kirsten,* she said to herself, *time to find some people.*

Chapter 3

Kirsten Stewart walked out of the safe house and base of operations in Inverness at ten o'clock in the morning. She'd managed to catch two hours of sleep after searching through the internet for details about Alastair Carlton's contacts. Justin Chivers had offered to sit beside Kirsten when everyone else had left. As much as his help may have been welcome, the obvious attention that would have come from the two of them being in the building alone was not, so Kirsten sent him on his way.

James Gunn and Alastair Carlton had been taken down to Glasgow where they would no doubt face more questions. For Kirsten, it was time to get on with the footwork. She had hoped to have a relaxing day since her main task of capturing Gunn and Carlton had been completed the previous night. With the extra information that had been spilled, however, work would carry on.

When she was with the police, she would get overtime. Kirsten could actually ask for extra pay to be signed off, but it seemed with the services, everything was fair game and you were not likely to get any extra pay no matter what was happening. Still, the pay was good and it opened up a different line of work that could be a lot more exciting, even more than being on the murder squad. As she made her way to her car, she recited the three names in her head, all contacts of Alastair Carlton, and all on a piece of paper in her back pocket with details of their addresses and last known places of employment.

The first address was in Inverness, out by one of the new builds on the southeastern side of the city. Kirsten made her way through several small roundabouts and past bunches of mothers with children and the occasional father, all heading to the school. As she turned into a small cul-de-sac, she pulled over and walked the extra fifty yards to make her way past Andy Target's house. Kirsten had read in a report that morning that he was a fixer like Alastair Carlton, and occasionally these people were known to get in touch with each other to pass on details of jobs and services required.

Kirsten made her way past, quickly glancing in all the front windows of the house. She could see a bald man inside, sitting watching television, and a woman in the background. They both seemed to have only arisen and were wearing dressing gowns, but beyond that, any further detail could not be acquired from the front of the building.

Glancing around her, Kirsten realized that she was in the cul-de-sac on her own, and quickly ran down the side of the house in between Andy Target's neighbours and his own driveway. At the rear of the house, she bent down low before peering in through the windows. The house was not immaculate but it certainly was in a tidy state. There were no signs of children—no small shoes, lunchboxes, bags left around, or any drawings on the wall. The only photos she could see were pictures of a man and a woman and occasional other adults.

Kirsten quickly made her way back to the car before opening

the boot, placing on a large luminous jacket that had the word 'Gas' written across the back. Nonchalantly, she walked up the front drive of Andy Target's and rapped on the door. The woman who opened it had long black hair and was probably old enough to be Kirsten's mother, but she was wearing a dressing gown that was cut just above the knee.

'Sorry to bother you,' said Kirsten. 'I'm from Scottish Gas. I just was following up an enquiry that was reported from this house by a Mr. Target—Andrew, is that correct?'

The woman looked blankly at Kirsten. 'I don't think so. He never mentioned anything to me.' She turned and shouted it into the front room, 'Andy, why is someone from the gas here? Did you make a report?'

'No, who the bloody hell is it?'

'Don't worry about it. I'll just tell her it wasn't you.' The woman turned back to Kirsten, shook her head. 'It can't have been us,' she said. 'We were only back last night. We've been out of the country for a month.'

'How lovely,' said Kirsten. 'Where'd you go?'

'Oh, it was holiday. He finally took me off to South Africa, on one of those safaris. It was lovely, so it was, but it can't have been us then.'

'Somebody's probably entered the details wrong in the computer,' said Kirsten. 'Not to worry.' Then she saw a man approaching from behind the door.

'All right, love. What is it? Something about a report?'

'Looks like somebody's got it wrong, put the address in by accident. I'm sorry to bother you, Mr. and Mrs. Target. Clearly it wasn't you. Your wife, sir, said that you've been away for a month on holiday.'

'Yes, that's right. It can't have been us.'

'That's all right. I'll check next door and beyond. Hopefully, they've put on the right street. Happens sometimes, postcodes and that, but sorry to have bothered you,' said Kirsten.

She turned away and made her way back to the car, pulling out some paperwork that was lying in the well of her front seat. After looking at it, she made her way to the house next door down to Target's and rapped on it to find that there was no one home. She made a visit to the house on the other side where an elderly lady was quite clear that she had made no report. Kirsten made her way back to the car, aware that Andy Target was looking out of the front window, watching her as she drove off.

That was the thing, you had to play out the whole charade. You could not go half measures. If she had not gone to either side of the house, he would have known she wasn't from the gas, but instead was probably from somebody in authority.

The second name on the list, an Ian Lackey, was easier to find. A quick phone call to the prison service showed he was still spending time down in Glasgow at Her Majesty's pleasure.

Kirsten drove to a small coffee shop and took a seat for fifteen minutes, drinking a rather bitter-tasting black variety of coffee that made her think she wasn't coming back to the shop again. Unrefreshed, but at least more switched on, Kirsten made her way to the next potential fixer, a man named Peter Harborough who lived in Dingwall, just beyond Inverness. His house was on the edge of Dingwall, a rather spectacular five-bedroom affair in the new build style.

After watching it for half an hour, Kirsten believed no one was home. After a quick, furtive scan around the house, and with no cars in the drive or garage, she believed he must have been out for the day. The man ran a jewellery shop in the centre of Dingwall, so Kirsten made her way in the car to park behind the main street.

The sky was overcast, and it began to rain. As she walked along the pedestrianized area, Kirsten looked at the town that was fighting like many others to keep its shops. The copious amount of charity vendors or other stores with 'closing down' in the window painted a grim picture that was rampant across the whole of the United Kingdom. Town centre life wasn't what it used to be.

Kirsten took a quick look at her phone before entering the jewellery store; she glanced again at the face of Peter Harborough. Once she had stepped inside, she could see him talking to a young woman. They were both dressed finely, he in a suit, she in a blouse and skirt. Kirsten made her way forward to one of the counters, and the woman approached her.

'I'm looking for something for my boyfriend,' said Kirsten. 'Some sort of simple chain.'

'Well, I'm afraid, ma'am, that I'm going to have to ask you to come back another time. There's been an unfortunate bereavement in the family.'

'Oh, dear. There isn't any way I could just quickly grab something?' asked Kirsten.

'No, I'm afraid not. That's the owner just behind me, Mr. Harborough, who needs to leave now. This means he needs to lock up. He was quite explicit to me when you came in that I needed to ask you to depart. I'm so sorry, but I'm sure you can understand the situation.'

'Someone close, is it?'

'I believe so. He didn't say exactly who, but he seems quite distraught.'

21

Kirsten looked over at the man. He seemed more agitated than distraught.

'Well, okay,' said Kirsten. 'I guess I'll have to go somewhere else, but thank you.' She walked out of the door, and took a seat outside in the street. She took off the jacket she was wearing, reversed it so it was a different colour, lifted out a baseball cap, and put it on her head. It was nothing significant, but at least it gave a different look if anyone glanced at her. Peter Harborough had seen her when she went into the shop, so Kirsten needed to make sure he didn't spot her again.

It was twenty minutes later when the man was at the front of the shop, locking up a grill across the window, and waving goodbye to his assistant. Another ten minutes later, he exited the shop, locked the front door, and began walking along the high street. Kirsten tailed him at a distance, and when she realized the man was going to an alternative car park within the town centre, she turned and ran to get her own car. Part of the trick of tailing someone was never to look as if you were in a rush, never to stand out, but she was, knowing she had to get her car round to the other car park and pick up Harborough's tail.

She reversed out of her space and made for the entrance of the car park, only to find a woman standing, kicking the wheel of her car as it blocked the entrance.

'What are you doing?' shouted Kirsten, rolling down the window. 'Can you move it? I'm in quite a hurry.'

'I can't move it. The stupid thing won't work,' said the woman.

Kirsten leapt out of the car and made her way over. 'Do you mind if I try?' she said, taking the keys off the woman and jumping into the front seat, ignoring the indignant look.

Kirsten put the keys in the ignition and tried to start the car. There was nothing. It was completely dead. Kirsten got back out of the front seat. 'Look, if you can get in the car now,' she said, 'I'll push you out of here. At least then you're not blocking anyone. You can call your AA or whoever else you've got, okay?'

'My boy's on his way. You don't have to rush. He'll be here in a minute. He'll probably be able to fix it. It's probably something I'm not doing.'

'The battery's dead,' said Kirsten, 'and I need to go. Go on, get in the car and I'll push you out of the way.' The woman went to remonstrate and Kirsten pulled a warrant card from inside her jacket. She didn't carry it when she was undercover, but as she was only doing basic tailing and not expecting to get frisked by anyone, it helped in times such as these.

'If you will kindly get inside the car, ma'am and drive, I'll push you clear.' The woman took a look at the badge and photograph that Kirsten was holding up and nodded quickly.

The car was heavy, a five-door saloon. Kirsten was grateful when the man from the car behind her joined her in pushing the woman's car to one side. She didn't wait to thank him. She jumped in her own car and sped away

Kirsten was stopped by two red lights before she could get to the car park she had left Peter Harborough in, and his car was gone. She remembered it as being a red sports coupe, and now having drawn a blank at the car park, she drove to his house. When she passed it, she saw the sports coupe and Peter Harborough packing something into the rear of it. It looked like a suitcase, and who knew what else? The behaviour was suspicious enough that Kirsten felt she should tail the man, but inside she had a dread feeling that this was going to be a long one. People rarely pack a suitcase, close down a jewellery shop, and just pop along round the corner. The two hours of sleep didn't feel like much now.

Peter Harborough left approximately five minutes later and Kirsten watched his car disappear from a side street. She picked up his tail and realized he was heading out of Inverness, climbing the hillside out of the city as the rain continued to beat down. She hoped he wasn't heading for Glasgow. She was not in the mood for a four hour drive, all that way, but this was the not-so-glamourous part of her job.

The cars cleared the summit of Slochd and Kirsten began to settle down for what she suspected would be a long drive. Popping open the glove compartment, she took out a boiled sweet, placed it in her mouth, and settled back, trying to think.

Kirsten really needed to see her brother in the daytime instead of her furtive night visits, but what did it matter when he didn't know her? Kirsten felt alone. It was during these quiet moments of the job that things started to get to her. Just how did you make friends in the services? People kept things so close to their chest. It wasn't like the Murder Investigation Team where they were all desperately sharing, desperately trying to find out the same thing, who a murderer was. Here, things were much more open, a much wider remit. Some of it, she didn't know.

A good half an hour later Kirsten watched Peter Harborough take the turnoff into Aviemore and a sigh of relief echoed from her mouth. At least he would stop driving soon, she thought. *Now, where are you off to?*

Chapter 4

Kirsten followed the car through the centre of Aviemore, and into a small estate at the rear of the town. Driving nonchalantly past, she watched Harborough park out in front of a small house which had been converted into flats. Then she pulled in nearby, adjusting her rear-view mirror, so she could watch what the man did. A middle-aged woman ran over to the car as Harborough stepped out, and flung her arms around him. Kirsten watched them as they embraced, but the man was looking around them, and quickly ushered the woman inside.

Stewart pulled out in the car again. She drove around the corner before parking up and changing her jacket. She threw on a blonde wig, and then changed her trousers from a bag in the rear of the car for a pair of jogging bottoms, and threw on a sweatshirt. She jogged round to the house where Peter Harborough had gone inside.

Kirsten forced herself to jog slowly, as if everything was a great effort, and as she reached the house of Peter Harborough, she bent over double, hands on her knees. But she was looking left and right, trying to gauge where the couple were in the house. The street was quiet, a typical suburb in the middle of the day. Most people would have been at work, children at school, and any activity would have been from delivery drivers or the post workers.

Happy no one was watching her, Kirsten cut across the lawn in front of the group of flats before crouching down and making her way along the wall at the side. Quietly moving to the rear of the house, she positioned herself under a window and then slowly took a small mirror on the end of a stem from her jacket. She extended the mirror, allowing her to see inside the room, and she froze when she saw two figures sitting across a table. It was Harborough and the blonde woman who had flung her arms around him outside. They seem to be having a heated discussion. Harborough was showing signs of distress.His hands kept running up through his hair. He would stand, then sit, then turn away from the woman. There were moments when he shouted and Kirsten caught a few words.

'It's out there. That's why.'

What was out there? The man very suddenly left his business in Dingwall. He had seen it as important to come here. She must have been his girlfriend, or a lover of some sort and now he was agitated again.

Kirsten was trying not to postulate too far ahead but wondered if this could this be the man who was arranging whatever was going to happen to the government or high society person. She was very in the dark, clutching at straws to work out what was going on. This could just as well be a domestic issue. Maybe this was an affair he was having. Maybe it was his wife, and she knew what was going on. Kirsten had been to his house and there was no other woman, at least not at the time.

The pair in the house continued to argue, and Kirsten

watched the man come up behind the woman, rubbing her shoulders. There suddenly seemed to be agreement. They wrapped their arms around each other, and then the woman headed out of the room.

Harborough made his way towards the rear of the house, and Kirsten collapsed the mirror, pocketed it and made her way around to the side, just as the rear door opened. Using the mirror again, she watched him step out of the back of the house, reach inside his jacket for some cigarettes, and light up. The man's hands were shaking, and his face wore all the cares of the world. If nothing else, he was worth watching, worth following.

Kirsten was now at the side of the house, a place where people from the road could see her. She quickly made her way back out, arriving onto the pavement, and began to jog off in the slow awkward fashion she had imitated before. On reaching the end of the street, she stopped, made her way behind some cars, crouched down low, and watched the house through a pair of small binoculars she had taken from the car.

These days, surveillance seemed to be everything. Kirsten had watched people for hours on end and had fought the urge when sitting in her car to have snack foods in front of her. She had watched all those American movies with the constant eating and chewing, and then wondered why the main stars never seem to put on any weight.

After half an hour, Kirsten stretched, picked up her phone from her pocket, and placed a call to Anna Hunt.

'Hello, Kirsten. It's Richard. Anna's tied up with something at the moment.'

Anna really must have been tied up with something, but clearly, she wanted an update as she had handed her phone to Richard. Maybe she was in a meeting. Richard was always around, close by, even if he was on the other side of a door, and it wasn't unusual for your phone call to be flipped to him.

'Richard, just tell her I might be onto something. One of the contacts, Peter Harborough checks out. He looks nervous, anxious. He's closed down his jewellery shop and he's on the move. I think he's with a girlfriend here in Aviemore. I have tried getting close, but I can't hear anything in the house, so I'm going to continue surveillance here. Tell Anna I'll give her something more when I've got it, but at the moment I would say this is a potential lead. Certainly, very suspicious and worth continuing to observe.'

'Okay,' said Richard, 'I'll pass it on to her. She's been chasing up leads all day herself, trying to find out if there was anything being said in groups or any chatter going about, but it's extremely quiet. It was a large hit going for somebody significant and it doesn't seem to have made it to the mainstream, so it must be being handled very well. Gunn and Carlton haven't said anymore, but in truth, I don't think Anna thinks they can help us any further. Gunn didn't know the person he was talking to. He was just wise and got out quick.'

'That's my take on it too, Richard, but we'll see how Peter Harborough checks out.'

Something caught Kirsten's eye down the street. A car had pulled up and two men stepped out, smartly dressed in dark suits, much as if they were going to a funeral.

'Got to go Richard, something's up.' Kirsten pocketed the mobile phone and began to take up her struggling jogger impersonation again. She ran along about ten steps then stopped, bent over huffing and puffing and then walked slowly along the street, her eyes constantly flicking over to the house of Peter Harborough's girlfriend.

The two men in suits knocked the door, and when Harborough opened it, Kirsten saw him trying to close it again quickly, but one of the men, the larger, seemed to have put his foot in the door. Harborough was pulled outside.

Kirsten was still at a distance, but it seemed like there was an argument going on, some pushing and shoving. Harborough was pushed up against the wall, and Kirsten ran across the street, so she could be on the nearer pavement when she passed the house. She began to wheeze as she got closer, faking that she was in trouble. She bent over the nearest hedge made a vomiting sound, and then turned back and let some drool drop from her mouth. She was now twenty yards from the house and could still see the two men holding Harborough up against the door. A finger was put in his face and a punch delivered to his stomach. The men turned away, but Harborough threw a punch into the back of the head of the largest man.

Kirsten knew how to punch. Apparently, Harborough didn't. She watched his hand recoil in pain. The large man seemed more shocked than hurt.He turned around and pushed Harborough back against the wall of the house. Another punch was delivered into the stomach, and a finger was pointed down at the now-doubled-up man.

'We'll know, we'll find out. They're not happy.' With that, the men marched back out to the street where they passed right in front of Kirsten. One of them looked down at her.

'Bitch can't even run, out of shape, hey?'

Kirsten watched the man's back as he got into his car. She would've loved to have taken them on for that comment, but she needed to see if she could tail them. In her mind, she made a note of the license plate and then began to limp on round to her car. She could tail the men, but then that would leave her prime target alone in a house. They had been agitated but they had made a decision and Harborough could make a move. That was what Kirsten was expecting, that he wasn't going to stay, especially now he had just been punched several times in the stomach.

When she made it to her car, the two men had driven off. She got inside, discarded her wig, drove the car down the street, turned around, came back up and passed the house where she saw Peter Harborough's car was still sitting. Looking up from the far end of the street, Kirsten watched with the binoculars, waiting for some movement.

Harborough had been hit quite hard. The blows to his stomach would have winded him, but he was probably not otherwise injured. He must have been desperate to have attacked that goon. Most people know they can't punch, so why take on somebody that's walking away? That must have been in anger or frustration.

Kirsten tried to surmise what had happened. Harborough had to be the contact, the go-between between Carlton and whoever it was that wanted a hitman. With the hitman arrested, Harborough was most likely afraid there would be investigations. If, as Carlton seemed to suggest, the target was high up, any potential leaks like this would be closed off, especially once confirmed. They were in the middle of a housing estate, so they would not do it right there and then; they would come back for him or they'd be subtle, waiting for an opportunity. Kirsten couldn't see anybody else near the house, so this must have just been a warning while investigations were going on. They probably told him not to leave, not to go anywhere.

Kirsten could feel her stomach churning. She was hungry. One of the downfalls of surveillance was you always ended up stuck in the same place for a long time. The car would usually have a selection of chocolate bars or health foods that she could munch into. Maybe a bottle of water somewhere, but she hadn't stocked up, and she was now beginning to regret it.

With the binoculars, looking down the street, Kirsten saw Harborough's girlfriend step out of the house and go to the next-door neighbour's. After a knock on the door, a man answered and keys were passed over.The woman looked nervous although the man she handed the keys to was smiling. She returned to the house and was inside for approximately five minutes before both Peter Harborough and she returned, walking past his car to another car that was parked at the side of the road. It was a small mini, black and cream, and looked fairly modern. A pair of fluffy dice hung down from the rear-view mirror and Kirsten wondered what possessed people to buy these things.

She had a cardboard cut-out of a pine tree hanging from her rear-view mirror, but it wasn't there for the smell. If she was working with someone else, she would make notes on the pine tree. If they were swapping shifts, she could indicate on it what the next person coming in needed to know.

When she had completed her initiation, she had trained to memorize car number plates, but it was also handy to write them down. At times she was forced to trust her memory, but why bother when something was there available for you?

Kirsten watched the couple get into the mini. As the woman went to start it, she stalled the car three times. Harborough put his hand across and they embraced before getting out of the car. Harborough took the wheel this time and the woman settled in beside him. With the binoculars, it was like Kirsten was in the car, and she could see the woman's eyes were wet with tears. Was this an escape? Was the woman scared?

When they pulled away, Kirsten started up her own car and kept her distance. She watched as the vehicle took the road back out to the A9 and took a left to continue south. Watching from four cars behind, Kirsten followed the couple as they headed off further into the mountains.

Chapter 5

H alf an hour south of Aviemore, Peter Harborough drove his mini off the A9 and into the mountains where it became harder for Kirsten to follow as they were the only two cars on the road. She had to keep her distance, catching only glimpses of him ahead. She nearly missed him as he turned down a sidetrack. As she was going on past and saw the sign for holiday homes with a quick flick of her head, Kirsten saw the brown and black of the mini disappearing in the distance. Reversing the car, she followed down the track that opened up into a set of six holiday homes. Kirsten arrived at a chain across the road, blocking her from going further. A sign indicated that the establishment was closed for the season due to refurbishments.

Kirsten stopped her own car before reversing it back up the road and found a small route into a group of trees allowing her to park her car out of sight. Donning her jacket, she made her way back across the road through the small forest that surrounded the holiday homes. Armed with her binoculars, she settled herself down amongst the trees and began to scan each of the homes. The mini had been left at one end of the small site and she was unsure which one the couple had made their way into.

It was only a short time before Peter Harborough made his way out, lighting up a cigarette and staring at the small track down to the site. His face showed wrinkles of worry. Kirsten saw his feet tapping as he took long drags of his cigarette, the wisp of smoke disappearing into the freshness of the forest. A light came on in the chalet behind him. The fixture itself was small, a single storey with a log exterior and in the background, Kirsten thought she saw the woman emerging from a bathroom, towel wrapped around her.

Peter returned inside and curtains were closed in various windows. Kirsten made her way back to her own car, happy that the two fugitives had taken refuge and were looking to bed down for a while. She followed the road back to the nearest service station and picked up sausage rolls and drinks to eat on the drive back. Within the hour, Kirsten was installed again in the forest watching the house. As afternoon went into evening, she lay there letting her eyes drop every now and again, going into a sentry sleep, letting the body rest but allowing the ears, the eyes, and the mind to stay alert. It was a practiced skill and one she'd be getting better at. When eight hours had passed and still there was no movement, Kirsten made her way back to the car again, driving off for further sustenance. She found a small fish and chip shop in a nearby village, satisfied her hunger, and made her way back. She must have been gone all of half an hour but when she returned, she noticed there were no lights on in the chalet. Maybe they'd gone to sleep?

Kirsten decided to take a closer look. Now that they were inside, she would need to be a lot quieter. She made her way across from the trees. Something seemed off. Each of the chalets were dark, which was fine. All the doors were closed.

34

This was as it should be. There was nothing else extraneous around the place. Then it clicked with her. There was no car.

Kirsten's hand moved towards her small handgun, and she froze in her current position scanning all around her, looking for any signs of other people. She made her way around the far end of the chalets, quietly taking up a position that allowed her to see along the rear of the chalets. Again, there was nothing different. Nothing untoward. The darkness was complete, making the shadows unfathomable. It may have been late summer, but the night was drawing in and the trees around the chalets blocked out what light remained.

Kirsten made her way along the rear, quietly creeping onto the wooden boards of the veranda of the house that the couple had been in. Carefully, she tried the rear door and was surprised to find it open. It was the tiniest of creaks and Kirsten pulled her gun, checking the interior and then looking all around her in case anyone was coming out of the trees from behind. She was in a dangerous position, open from the rear and not knowing what was going to be in front of her. She stepped inside and closed the door gently behind her. The key for the door was still on the lock and she turned it. She didn't want anyone following her in. Yes, it would block her escape route out but she was feeling very exposed and thought she'd escape from a different angle.

Slowly, Kirsten crept along the hall, her back sliding tightly to it, her gun trained into the darkness. There were no signs of life in the house except for the occasional creak. The noise was not the floorboards, but the building itself, those routine noises you hear in the dead of night in any building, masked during the day by louder more conspicuous movement.

Kirsten reached the door that would lead into what she

thought would be the main room. Having previously looked through the window with her binoculars when studying the house earlier in the day, she knew there was a small sofa and a television. As she neared the door, she realized it was open, and taking out her mirror she extended it round the corner. She couldn't see anyone there so she withdrew it and stepped cautiously around the door.

The mirror had lied and in the dark, she saw a figure on the floor. Before stepping to it, Kirsten first scanned the room, her weapon before her, and then she shuffled close to the figure. It seemed prone so she gave it a tap with her foot on the head and it rolled from one side to the other. There was long hair and in the dark Kirsten thought it to be blonde. It looked like Peter Harborough's girlfriend had suffered a rather grisly end. But Kirsten couldn't check that right now. She had to make sure the rest of the house was clear.

Kirsten made her way through to the kitchen at the rear, again finding nothing. There was one other room, a small bedroom, but it didn't look as if it had been touched. There was a case of clothes on the far side, unopened, with just a simple t-shirt lying on the top. She made her way back into the front room and kneeled down to look into the face of Harborough's girlfriend. The eyes were closed, the neck lying to one side, and she realized why when she had kicked the head it had moved so gently. The throat had been slashed and there was a copious amount of blood drying on the floor.

Kirsten checked the wound. It was brutal, but it was also very neat. This had not been done by a hacking butcher, but rather by somebody who knew how to use a knife. Kirsten walked around the room looking for something, any sort of clue of what had happened, but there were just the holiday home items. There was no extra piece of paper, no books, no iPads, nothing that didn't belong except for the clothes in the other room. Kirsten made her way through to check the case. The t-shirt she recognized as the one that had been worn by the woman on the way there. When she unzipped the case, she saw an array of clothes. A wet towel was lying on the far side of the bedroom.

She would need to go outside, check for tyre tracks to see what sort of vehicle had been there, if indeed any. She could have a skirt around and see if she could find footprints. Kirsten slowly made her way to the rear door, opening it first and looking out before then stepping through and closing it behind her. They had been and gone, and they had taken Peter Harborough with them.

The wood above Kirsten's hands splintered with the bang of a gun. It was now reverberating through the night but Kirsten didn't wait to find out where the shot had come from. She raced to the corner of the house to get out of the line of fire. Another shot rang out. Kirsten reckoned that this shot had come from behind her. As she cleared the corner, she peeked back to see if anything was moving.

A figure in the dark was running towards the house. Kirsten pulled her weapon with its silencer and fired. With the sound of the bullet hitting something, she knew she had missed, but the figure turned, running back to the cover that it had emerged from. Kirsten doubled round to the far side of the house in case the attacker emerged towards the path that lead to the road. She saw the figure moving, and rather than fire this time, she ran over towards the trees.

Kirsten saw that the person was going to reach the road before she could cut them off, so she fired into the air. Despite having a silenced weapon, the small noise still echoed in the night. When the person backed away quickly into the undergrowth at the side of the site, Kirsten wasn't sure if they knew where she was and she stepped as lightly as she could. The forest debris made it almost impossible for her to tread silently.

Kirsten made her way along until she got to where her part of the forest met the path out to the main road. She could see a figure half moving out of trees ahead but she wasn't sure if it was a person or even possibly just a branch in motion. Stepping lightly and holding her breath, she made the next twenty yards in under five seconds. Reaching around, she put her hand on what she thought would be a shoulder, but when she touched what she thought should be skin, all she felt was wood.

There was a crack of a twig on the ground. Kirsten threw herself down as a gunshot went over her head from what must have been nearly point-blank range. She couldn't run. The shooter was too close, possibly ready to make another shot, so with her ears ringing, she turned and threw herself forward, catching someone in the midriff. Together they tumbled to the ground, Kirsten's gun falling to one side. As she stood up, she saw an arm being extended towards her, a weapon in the hand and she kicked it hard, catching the wrist. The hand snapped away to one side and she kicked it again, driving it against a tree stump, causing the weapon to fall. The person lashed out at her, catching her shoulder and she stumbled backwards, clattering into a tree. Kirsten knew she had to spin, had to turn, had to get back on her feet, but she was slow. She could hear the other person rising. Surely, they'd have their gun soon, but where was hers? Somewhere on the ground?

Kirsten ducked behind a tree and could hear the next gunshot going off. It was farther away than the last one and her ears were still ringing from the sound, but nothing hit her. Then she heard crunching small twigs and leaves as her assailant ran away. Looking quickly from behind the tree, she saw a man disappearing out of the wood to the small path. Kirsten looked down for her gun, knowing that following him would be ridiculous if he was still carrying a weapon. It took her about fifteen seconds to find it and when she made it out to the path, she saw the man running and knew it would be a struggle to get a decent shot.

So, Kirsten followed him, legs pumping, ears still ringing. She found herself swaying from one side to the other as she ran, but she wanted to make sure the man did not get away. All their leads had gone. Peter Harborough was missing, his girlfriend dead. If this man got away, what else would they have?

As she approached the end of the road, she saw a car pull up, no lights on. The man opened the passenger door, got in, and the car sped away. By the time Kirsten got there, the car was long gone and she hadn't managed to read the number plate. Her ears were recovering but there was still a dull consistent sound going through them. Her body felt exhausted but checking herself over she realized she was okay. There'd be a bruise on her shoulder, but nothing had hit her. No bullets, no scratches from that.

The gunfire had been loud and people would come. Quickly, she made her way along the road and found her car. Sitting down inside, she grabbed the water she had bought and gulped it down. Then she picked up her phone to ring her boss, and hurriedly relayed the details of the situation.

'This all seems to have gone rather south, doesn't it? But we're onto something. Clearly, you failed to tag the intruder and bring him in,' said Anna.

'You could try the number plate of the guys I saw earlier on at the house, see if that brings up anything.'

'We will do, but you get out of there. I don't want you there when police arrive. At the moment, we're on the right side of this and they won't know who's involved and who's come snooping. Could have been Harborough's friend for all they know. We'll keep it that way. Let the police discover it. You can't do anything for the girl now.'

Kirsten thought back to the body lying on the floor. She knew that Anna was right. Best to keep going at this from the dark. Part of her imagined her old team now arriving at the site in the morning, puzzling on what had happened, Jona the forensic lead, finding bullets here and there. Maybe Anna would have a word higher up. Maybe she wouldn't. That was the thing, you never quite knew what was going to happen, how Anna wanted to play it. She liked to be operating from a position of denial. Never liked her operatives anywhere close to where a body was found by the public.

Kirsten turned the ignition and drove her car back to her small flat in Inverness. She had moved from where she had lived while working in the murder investigation team. Now she lived on a rather cheap estate. The top flat of a rather rundown place. As she climbed the stairs, she could hear the junkie on the floor below. Once inside her small bedsit, she turned on some music and smiled as she heard a light jazz trumpet playing. She stripped off her sweaty clothes and made her way into her shower. Her body absorbed the heat from the sprinkling water, and she wished the jet was more powerful.

She applied shampoo and realized her hands were shaking. If she had not ducked? If she hadn't . . . Quickly she stepped out of the shower, flipped open the lid of the toilet, and vomited. After flushing, she stepped back into the shower and lowered herself to the basin and sat cross legged as the water washed over her. *If I hadn't ducked*, she thought.

Chapter 6

The buzz of her mobile phone vibrating on the table caused Kirsten to wake. She fumbled her hand on top of the bedside table until she eventually found it and pulled it into bed with her. If this was Anna, she was not going to be happy. Kirsten had been up half the night, she'd cried for quite a while of it, and now she wanted to sleep.

Kirsten desperately looked at the screen, but everything was blurred. She reached for her glasses, swaying them across, sliding them up her nose, as she had always been prone to do. The trouble with using contacts was you got used to them being there and then when you woke up in the morning, they were absent. It took a moment for the brain to register why you were not seeing clearly.

Staring at the screen, Kirsten cursed. While it was not unreasonable for the bank to send her a notification about a new statement being released, she really didn't need it at this time of the morning. She wished she could put the phone back on block, just take away all the important messages and be allowed to sleep, but the business she was in prevented that. Sometimes she was called during the night or something important came in unexpectedly, and she couldn't take the risk of the phone not being available.

Placing the phone back on the desk, Kirsten sat up in bed and felt a slight chill. She liked the house to be cool, never warm, but when she got out from underneath the duvet, she felt it. If it were a routine workday, Kirsten would have popped on her running gear and taken a good two to three-mile run before coming back and showering and sitting down to breakfast.

Having been awake half the night, Kirsten was not interested in running, but instead stumbled across her small bedsit to the kitchen where she poured a bowl of cereal. She was three mouthfuls in when her hand began to shake. She brought her left hand across to her right in an attempt to stop it, but in the end, she put the spoon back in the bowl, unable to control it coming to her mouth.

She found her ears beginning to ring, not like they had the previous night, not when the gun was close, but a form of tinnitus. *Come on, pull yourself together*, she thought; *he missed. He missed me*, but her hand refused to stop shaking. She stood up and made her way back into the shower. It had only been a few hours ago that she'd taken one, but she thought that cleaning her body would occupy her and give her hand something to do, something where if it shook, it didn't matter.

Twenty minutes later, she was sitting back at her bowl, clean, refreshed, but still unable to control the rampant hand that had spilled the milk that she saw was sitting beside the bowl. Kirsten left her flat dressed in jeans and a t-shirt, her hair under a baseball cap with a leather jacket slung over her shoulder. The walk to the office would have been far for her so instead, she caught the bus and was soon sitting behind the desk she had seen two nights ago.

The office was empty, as Anna Hunt had promised. Kirsten

buried herself in the computer. This is what she had been so good at on the murder investigation team. She started to track down Peter Harborough, looking first at his jewellery shop, trawling through accounts. It didn't take her long to come up with a name. The firm of Mitchell and Sons lawyers sprung out from the many bills.

Kirsten picked up the phone, calling a number she used to call her work-home. In part, she was hoping to speak to Ross, a former colleague, or McGrath, her boss, or even the DI himself, but none were available. She struck out, as they were all unavailable. No doubt, they were looking at a woman with her throat cut, farther down in the highlands. But she was familiar with the sergeant there and asked if the name of John Mitchell meant anything to him.

'John Mitchell, the lawyer? We get him in here a lot, usually with the more serious criminals, the ones that really don't want to be caught. They say if Mitchell doesn't get them out, sometimes that could be the end of it. A dead-end lawyer, you can say. Someone you've really got to put your trust in.'

As Kirsten walked along the street, going to her favourite donut shop, the name ran over in her head. Mitchell, dead-end lawyer. You had to trust him. When she had stocked up with her raspberry glazed donut and a black cup of coffee, Kirsten sat on the bus to Inverness town centre. The offices of Mitchell and Sons were in one of the old town centre buildings, four stories high, with large windows at the top, and the dark, damp-looking stonework that had once been all the rage downtown. That was the thing about this type of building: you could never change it. It was as if the city aged around it. Yes, there was tarmac on the streets and there were no more cobbles, but it felt like it should be. Even the modern signage down below couldn't take away the grandeur of the building.

Kirsten consulted her phone, looking at a photograph with John Mitchell. Upon arriving in the street of his offices, she promptly plonked herself at the coffee house on the far side of the road. She took out a paperback she'd been reading. It was trashy, half erotic, and in truth, she was barely reading it, but she found that when she held the book up, no one wanted to speak to her. The man on the cover with the impressive chest touching the woman with the heaving bosom told a picture of Kirsten that a lot of people didn't want to disturb.

She placed her phone before her in the book and began reading from the screen various newspaper articles about the firm of Mitchell and Sons. The man's name seemed to appear in a number of court cases, but there was nothing strange about the business itself. Everything looked above board. He was the lawyer everyone came around to once they had been caught by the police.

Whilst reading, Kirsten kept an eye on the entrance to the tall building that led up to the offices of the lawyer. She changed coffee shops three times, blessing the fact that apart from charity shops, they seemed to be the most predominant thing on the high street. After about five hours, her waiting was rewarded and she saw John Mitchell leave the building. He was dressed in a dapper grey suit, a briefcase at his side, and walked as if he didn't have a care in the world.

Kirsten folded up her book and tucked it into her pocket and left the coffee house, watching her target from a distance. As she made her way along the street, Kirsten became aware of two men ahead of her. When Mitchell turned around various corners, a technique to lose people, she realized they were still following. Cutting up through a side alley, and approaching from a different angle, she was able to stand on the corner as Mitchell walked past and get a good look at the two men who were tailing him.

As she continued her tail some distance back, she picked up the phone and called in, once again getting Richard Lafferty on the call.

'Anna is talking to people. What's up?'

Kirsten relayed the information, advising Lafferty that she was still tailing the potential suspect, although she was getting nervous because of the two men following.

'I think they may have killed Harborough. They certainly roughed him up. If they are not the executioners, they are certainly the welcoming committee.'

'You want me to interrupt her?'

'Definitely.'

'Last time, she was pissed. I got the broadside from it. Do you know that? I mean, you said to do it, but I was the one that got into trouble for it.'

Kirsten could hear Lafferty laughing in the background. 'Just do it. I don't know how long this tail is going to last. I need an answer before I get there.'

Kirsten continued to walk, the phone to her ear. She saw John Mitchell continue to try and throw his tail off. She wasn't sure if he was aware they were behind him or if indeed he was just running a standard route, but it was complex and she certainly couldn't be seen again by him. After all, he'd already passed her by. People who are running things like this, who make tails that are hard to follow would remember a face. Kirsten stepped aside and took her contacts out. Removing her glasses from her pocket, she continued to tail but tied her hair up behind her in a ponytail, tucking it up under the hat so it looked like she had short hair.

'You still there?' asked Lafferty.

'Go.'

'She said, stay on it. Doesn't want to spook anybody but she said you have to stay with him. See where he goes, see who he sees, but don't let anything happen to him. If it gets too hot, bring him in.'

'Understood,' replied Kirsten. *It's all right for her*, she thought. *Just look after him. Let him meet whoever. Somebody takes a pot shot. You're then trying to run away in the middle of all the heat.'* As it was, John Mitchell got into a taxi and was closely followed by another taxi containing two men. This taxi in turn was followed by a young female. Being in the last of the taxis, Kirsten had to stop well short.

When she got out, she found herself in a residential area of the town, just up the hill past the castle. The man had barely travelled any distance, but he'd done so in such a circuitous route that it felt like she had enjoyed a good workout. Kirsten was able to stand at a distance, binoculars at the ready, watching as the two men from the taxi in front of her approached what she believed to be John Mitchell's house. There were two large pillars at the front door and the building looked like it contained six or seven bedrooms.

Kirsten watched as the door opened and Mitchell was pulled out. There was the sort of roughing up she'd seen back in Aviemore, a few punches to the stomach before the men left. When they didn't return, Kirsten stayed in the street, now holed up behind the hedge in a house she believed was unoccupied.

Later in the evening, Kirsten saw a white car pull into the drive of Mitchell's house. A tall, brunette-haired woman emerged and was greeted at the door by John Mitchell. Kirsten wondered if she was going to see a repeat of what had happened previously. *Was the man going to get ready to run? Had he been threatened? Was this a girlfriend or was it the wife?*

According to the records that she obtained online, John Mitchell was married to Margaret Mitchell, but she had no photograph of the woman. When she saw the couple sit down to dinner, Kirsten took the chance to grab a taxi back to her own house and pick up her own car. When she returned to the street with a bag of chips in her hand, having parked her own car around the corner, Kirsten made her way back to the seemingly abandoned house, sitting down behind the hedge, making herself hidden from any passers-by.

It was an art form, staying quiet, digesting her food, making sure she didn't rustle anything. Several people passed along the street but none of them looked her way. None of them saw a hedge worth investigating. Why would they? It was just a hedge and there was nothing untoward in the street.

Kirsten was almost dozing off, when at midnight John Mitchell left the house. She caught his car and the registration—a flashy, white Porsche and quickly she ran for her own car around the corner. It took her two or three streets of hunting before she caught the car again and settled in to tail him to wherever he was heading. He started out towards the airport and when he broke off on a route to Ardersier, Kirsten began to get uncomfortable.

There was a set of woods just before the airport, but the Porsche turned away before that, parking up at the golf club that sat on the shores of the Moray Firth, the broad expanse of water that ran under the large bridge that took the Inverness road over to the Black Isle.

Passing the golf club, Kirsten was able to park up a small distance away, so near that she almost ran into John Mitchell coming out of his own car and starting to head across the course. The difficulty Kirsten was enduring was that of being at a golf course, and a links one at that. There were hardly any trees. She was struggling to see any, but Kirsten remembered her training and she kept low, always with some terrain behind her.

The course descended down towards the shore. As he was crossing one of the fairways, a small shout came out and John Mitchell turned back up one of the holes towards the green at the end. The flag had been removed and a large circle of green seemed to have only one person on it. In the dark, it was hard to tell if it was a man or a woman, but the figure stood impassive as Mitchell walked towards it. Kirsten watched Mitchell's gait. He certainly didn't look scared. Rather, Mitchell carried himself authoritatively as if he was on his way to sort something out. Given the people that he worked for, Kirsten wondered if the man was wise.

Kirsten was fifty yards away. Even though she was crouched down, she needed to skirt a bunker, so she wouldn't appear as a shadow in the white sand. After getting to the other side of it, she scanned the green, and there saw the figure now extend an arm. Mitchell had stopped. He then turned and began to run, but he was only twenty yards away from the person on the green. There was a small flash of light, but no resounding crack, so the weapon must have been silenced. Mitchell spun.

Kirsten drew her weapon, firing at the person on the green. With silenced weapons, it was a bizarre game of cat and mouse. You could tell shots had been fired, but it was almost like they were done delicately. Kirsten had the better aim, for the person on the green was hit to some degree, not seriously, but enough so that they turned and ran. Kirsten kept an eye on the retreating figure as she made her way over to Mitchell, who was lying on the ground.

'John Mitchell, listen to me; put your good arm up around my neck, and we run.'

'I'm not going with—'

'Shut up and do it. If I don't get you out of here, you're dead.' Kirsten was unsure if this information was correct, but there was certainly a strong possibility. She was no longer crouching, instead lifting herself to the full height, bearing the weight of the man as his arm went around her neck. For such a small stature, she had a good engine inside and she certainly felt as if she was carrying most of the weight of the man. They stumbled across into the car park, looking to head out of the rear of it and run to where Kirsten had parked her car. She saw a figure up ahead and instantly threw John Mitchell off to one side. A shot whizzed past them. Kirsten was unsure whether it was beside her, over the top or somewhere else. Again, she drew her weapon, firing into the dark from where the man had come from. This time, Mitchell was up on his feet, trying to run away.

'Stay with me,' said Kirsten. 'He won't come for me. He'll come for you, and you don't have a weapon.' Flanking her injured party, Kirsten fired again when she saw movement in the dark. When she saw it move off to her left, she knew it was moving away from where she wanted to go.

'Run out of the car park, round the back. That's my car there. Get into the passenger seat. Go.' Kirsten ran backwards as John Mitchell ran for his life. She fired several times before turning around herself, running hard towards the car. When she reached it, she jumped inside, taking the keys from her pocket and starting it without a thought. Mitchell had only just got in when she drove off, the door slamming tight beside him.

'Do you think we're clear?' said Mitchell. As if on cue, the back window exploded and Kirsten saw a bullet crack in the front as well.

'Get your head down, and don't lift it up until I say.' Kirsten sped the car up with certainty. She knew the road. Up ahead, she could take a right and head back to the main route into Inverness. Knowing that she was clear, she picked up her phone and dialled an emergency contact.

'Yes, Chivers,' said a voice in the other end.

'I'm coming in hot,' said Kirsten. 'And I'll need the doctor.'

'I like the sound of that. Always thought you were hot, myself.'

'Chivers!' Kirsten's tone was furious. It was nothing less than what she expected from the man. If he didn't have the computer skills he had, he would have been fired by any decent employer.

'The doctor, okay, how long?'

'I'll be there in about twenty minutes. Injury to the arm. Bullet wound. Don't think it's inside. I think it nicked. Possible flesh wound.'

'Understood.'

Kirsten switched off the phone. 'You can come up now,' she said to Mitchell.

'Who are you?' he said.

'I'm just a friend, Mr. Mitchell. One of your friends. Can't have a good lawyer like you getting taken out, can we? After you've done so much for us.'

'Do you know why they came for me? Do you know who came for me?'

'I think Carlton was talking. He's got Peter Harborough in trouble. I thought they'd come after you. That's why we're keeping you safe. Sit back, relax. We'll get you out of the country before tomorrow.'

Kirsten watched the man smile and lay back. That was the thing. The people that worked in these ranks had many, many friends; maybe they believe they would come to their aid. Kirsten thought differently. She thought that many of them would just dump them. But a story had been told and he'd taken it hook, line, and sinker, but what use would he be? What did he know? They'd find out in the next couple of hours.

Chapter 7

Kirsten was listening to the kettle boil, realizing that the sun was about to come up and knowing that she hadn't slept well in several days. Anna Hunt had driven up from Glasgow as soon as she heard about the incident at the golf course. Upon arrival, she had demanded coffee. The house Kirsten was in was a partially derelict affair, on the edge of Inverness, located on a street that most of the residents had left. A pair of rather drab curtains blocked out what sunlight would come and kept prying eyes from looking in, and seeing the run-down sofa, on which trembled John Mitchell.

The man had been fortunate; the gunshot wound was just a graze. Although the skin was intact, his nerves were not. He was jittery, babbling, talking constantly about going into protection and getting away from the country. Kirsten had said nothing to the man, except to sit and wait, for her boss would be there soon enough. She was the one who could talk about all of that. But first John would have to come up with something, information that would assist Kirsten and her team.

The steam rose from the top of the kettle and the switch

clicked, indicating it had done its job. There were three chipped mugs, and Kirsten picked out the one with the smallest chip for herself. After all, she'd done all the work. Richard was out in the hall, ever available to his boss. At this moment is was safer for him to take up a position that could still protect Anna, while at the same time leave him out of the conversation taking place in the sitting room. Filling up three mugs with instant black coffee, Kirsten carried them through and saw Anna peering out a grimy window.

'I don't think they're here for you yet, John,' she said. 'But they will be. They've come already, and will finish what they started.' Kirsten watched John Mitchell's thumbs twiddling as his hands stuck fast together. His shoulders were slumped. The man was gazing up at Anna Hunt who had turned and was now staring back at him, expressing her conviction that the people with the guns would come again.

'That's coffee,' said Kirsten, placing one down in front of Mitchell on the floor. The carpet was a faded orange colour and had seen much better days. In fact, the whole room had. The wallpaper had the occasional peeled piece and there were a range of pictures of people Kirsten didn't know. Anna wouldn't have known them either. The place was decorated to give the impression that somebody actually lived here, albeit in a form of squalor.

'Drink your coffee, John,' said Anna. She looked out of place with her crisp skirt, high heels, and silk blouse. She should have been in an office like some high-powered executive. Kirsten was more in keeping with where they were now, the rough and ready look and the baseball cap still on her head.

'You drink your coffee, John. I'll be back in a minute.' Anna Hunt nodded to the door indicating that Kirsten should follow her. 'Richard, step inside for a minute. Keep an eye on our guest.' With that, Richard Lafferty exchanged places with the two women. Once the door had closed, Kirsten prepared herself for the questions that would follow.

'So, what was the shooter like?' asked Anna.

'Believe it was male, possibly just under six foot. Didn't really get much more of a look. Sounded like a standard firearm. Nothing special,' said Kirsten.

'So not a specialist brought in, not our hitman we are looking for then?'

'Well if it is, he's a pretty shoddy one,' said Kirsten. 'You've got your guy coming on the golf course. He's walking up. You're on the green and it's open country. Yes, it's the middle of the night, but, hey, it's not like you couldn't see him. Hits his arm. Rubbish shooting.'

'Could you have taken him down from that distance?'

Taking him down. She said it so lightly, thought Kirsten. Guns had never been in Kirsten's repertoire, but she had to learn when she joined the service. Yes, she had fired them in anger, but so far, she had never killed anyone, never had to shoot someone in such a way as to take them down. She knew how to do it, but she found Anna's way of talking about it so cold. As if it's just part of the job, and yes, it was part of the job, but it wasn't a part that Kirsten liked. She wondered how her old boss, Macleod, would have thought of her if she had to take someone down.

'I could have made that shot, and I could have made it easily.'

'So, is someone trying to sort it out for their boss? Someone not that clever? Is someone not happy that we're going to know someone's been brought in? Someone to deal with a serious target.'

'Sounds like a bottom feeder clearing up or being instructed to by someone at the lower ends,' said Kirsten.

'It sounds to me like this is worth pursuing,' said Anna, 'and as of now, it's your top priority. We'll get what resources we can to you, but you're going to have to run this one on the quiet. No big fanfare. They don't need to see us coming. We need the intelligence, Kirsten, and we need it much sooner rather than later. If this is a top target, and if this thing is for real, I'm going to look pretty bad if we don't find out who it is and where and when.'

'I take it the other two haven't said much.' Kirsten was referring to James Gunn and Alastair Carlton. Anna shook her head and said nothing.

'Neither have we had any information on Peter Harborough. In saying that, I don't expect to find him, not unless some diver or submarine picks him out of whatever bit of the sea they've dumped him into. As I see it, our main lead's in there, and he looks pretty shaken, so I'm going to put the screws on him, see what we can find out, and then I'm letting you loose, Kirsten. This will be your first biggie. Don't screw it up on me, okay?'

Kirsten Stewart had practiced mixed martial arts fighting for years. Sometimes she stepped into the octagon and looked across and felt a shiver run down her spine. Sometimes she was practically terrified, but the one thing she could do was keep her face that said, 'I'm here to destroy you.' That face was now being displayed despite the nervousness she felt about taking on a case of this magnitude. When she had worked on the murder team with Macleod, there were situations like this, figuring things out against the clock before someone died, but Macleod was running the operation. He was in charge. She was merely part of the team. Here in the service, it seemed to work differently. Maybe it was easier to dispose of you if you got it wrong. Less of a corporate-blame attitude. Best to get it right then.

'Well, we'd better get something of interest then,' said Kirsten, smiling at her boss as she opened the door. 'Shall we?'

John Mitchell was still sitting on the sofa, but his head was now in his hands. Richard looked up as the two women entered, gave a simple nod, and stepped back outside into the hallway beyond.

'Mr. Mitchell, or shall I say, John? You're right in it, aren't you? Right in the middle of it.'

'Get me out. I'll tell you whatever you want to know, but you've got to get me out.'

'Well, I'll see what I can do for you,' said Anna, 'but all of it depends on what you know.'

'You've got to promise to get me out,' said Mitchell.

'You are the one who's on a golf course in the middle of the night getting shot at. The police would love to know what you were doing there. I'd love to know what you were doing there, but more than that, I'd love to know the story behind it. I'd love to know why a lawyer feels the need to be there, or anyone feels the need to bring their lawyer to such a location in the dead of night. You know a lot, don't you? You know too much, Mr. Mitchell.'

John Mitchell looked up, and Kirsten could see tears in his eyes.

'I didn't want to know. He didn't need to tell me. It's his way of protecting himself. It was his way of covering off.'

'Go on,' said Kirsten, 'because so far, you haven't said anything.'

'And I don't know that much. That's the craziness of it,' said

John Mitchell. 'He told me so little. He took me out to lunch and there, in the middle of talking about his girlfriend, he says to me, "There's somebody coming, accurate, very good from a distance, going to sort it out, good money but high risk." At least high-risk with Peter, that's the feeling I got. He said he'd try to get the usual mob to do it but they'd run. They weren't happy, so he'd had to go abroad, had to get somebody special.'

'Who did he get?' asked Anna.

'He's not stupid.'

'I guess he wasn't,' said Anna, 'but he is dead. I mean, you know that, don't you? I know that—his girlfriend's dead anyway,' said Anna, 'My colleague saw her, not a pretty sight. Peter was not with the body. I guess she probably got it lucky. Somebody appeared from behind, cut her throat, and she was dead in a few seconds. Probably didn't even know what hit her. They'll take him away, won't they? Do you know what they do to people like that?'

Mitchell held his head in his hands again. 'Don't want to know. I want away, you hear me? I want away.'

'They might beat you, not with anything nice either. Iron bars, whatever. Tie your hands up, have you hanging, take a kick at you. When I say a kick I mean, like a half-hour or so. Get some knives and do a bit of training, work out all over your body. They might even do nastier stuff, cut things off. I've seen plenty of that before. You don't want to get caught with them. You don't want to have angered them, John.'

'I said you need get me out of here.'

'What do you know? You've told me somebody big, some-body coming from abroad. That's it.'

'That's all he told me,' said Mitchell, almost shouting.

'Keep your voice down,' said Kirsten, 'there's people sleeping in the street.' Mitchell threw her a glance, but Kirsten just smiled.

'That's all he told you? You're seriously telling me that he takes you out to dinner and just drops a couple of lines like that. Why drop a couple of lines?'

'Insurance policy. He now knows that I know something. Of course, he'll let them know that I know a bit, so if they come for him, he can pick up a phone and I have to help him. I have to get us both out because he'll tell them if they get a hold of him; he'll tell them that I'm involved. Somebody told them. That's why I'm on a golf course in the middle of the night. Told to come, for people you don't refuse. I was looking to try and negotiate my way out, but I know nothing.'

'You don't shoot people who know nothing,' said Anna.

'They do shoot people if they don't know what they don't know. They reckon he could have told me everything. You see, he called. Peter Harborough tried to call me but I've been away. I'm only just back in the country, off on holiday. I saw his call but didn't respond, didn't want to respond, was having a good time.'

'Where were you?' asked Kirsten.

'Spain, on a yacht with a client. He was entertaining me, all the booze I wanted, all the drink I wanted, and the woman I wanted. Why would I pick up a phone call from that arsehole? Then I get back, and I get a call from some people.'

'What people?' asked Anna

'The people that Peter deals with.'

'Names,' said Anna.

'I am his lawyer, he doesn't tell me bloody names. Why would he do that? And I wouldn't damn well listen. If he started giving me names, I'd drop him. I'd walk from him. He knew that as well.'

'He let you know a piece about something big,' said Kirsten. 'He dropped you in it. He dropped you in it hoping you would come and save him, and you were too busy on a yacht.'

'Too busy on a yacht?' said Anna, 'She's right, isn't she? Too busy on a yacht playing hide the sausage with someone, and then you walk back into this.'

'But you've got to get me out of it, you've got to get me on the plane out of this country.'

'It's okay; you can end up in prison,' said Anna. 'We'll look after you there.'

Mitchell laughed, 'Prison? That would be a death sentence from these people. They'd get me there, give it a week. No, I want out.'

'But you haven't given me anything,' said Anna. 'Why would I go to all the trouble? You're just a low-life scum, and you expect me to save you . . . for what? Because there's something big coming? I know that already. I got that off people who didn't even know what the job was. Didn't know the people that were coming for them. They're going to prison. I'm sure I can find someone to put you there.'

Kirsten was not sure that Anna had anything on the man to put him in prison. After all, all they'd done was tail him and he was shot, but the mere mention of prison was freaking John Mitchell out. He stood up, lurched towards Anna.

'You've got to help me; you'll damn well help me.'

With that, he made a grab for her throat. Anna Hunt rarely moved fast. In the short time that Kirsten had known her, she had never seen the woman have to react. She had always stood in a room of people, commanding them, telling them what to do. When she had been out in the field, it was at the end of hostilities, and Kirsten had always wondered if Anna had been a field operative.

In a flash, Anna grabbed the man's wrist, spun him around, and pulled the arm up behind his back. Another hand took his shoulders and drove him down to his knees.

'I don't have to do jack for you,' said Anna. 'You're going to sit here, and you're going to write down every bit of information you can for me. Every contact, every address you know of Peter's. Any passwords, all contacts, all meetings, and if I get to the end of it and I think, "Do you know what? He's actually not done bad there," I might try and look after you. If you don't, I'll let you walk back out of this place. You'll be back out in the open sea where any big fish could swallow you up.'

'Plenty of sharks out there, John,' said Kirsten.

'Kirsten, go and get Mr. Mitchell a pad and a pencil, and then I think we're going to leave him for an hour, see what that mind of his can jog up. Don't think about trying anything stupid, plenty of fixtures here you could injure yourself on, Mr. Mitchell, but our friend will be in the room and he'll make sure you don't come to any harm.'

'Richard,' shouted Anna. Richard walked into the room, 'Take a seat,' said Anna, 'Mr. Mitchell here has got some writing to do, just make sure that's what he does.' With that, Anna made her way out of the room, indicating with a finger that Kirsten should follow. The women retired to the kitchen at the rear of the house where Kirsten recharged their cups with fresh coffee.

'We'll see what he's got,' said Anna, 'and if it's good, you're off and running. He looks properly scared, which is not a good thing. It means there's some very heavy-handed people. For what he knows, which is probably nothing, you could just put the frighteners on him. That man is not going to speak. There's no way he would speak. He knows the score but this is so big that he's not prepared to take the risk. Or somebody up above him knows it's big to people higher up and they've sent people down, amateurs albeit, to close the door before the horse bolts.'

'So, you're saying I need to climb up the chain?'

'Exactly. Find a starting point, whatever it is, and work your way up until we find what's at the top. Like I say, do it on the quiet, me only, report it to me only. I don't often question the integrity of the department or who we work for, but I'd be naïve to think that nothing ever gets out, and with something this big, the last thing we need is plans being switched once we're on the tail of someone. So, it's me only, understood, Kirsten?'

'Absolutely.'

'You best get some shut-eye then, you haven't had much. I'll let him stew for a couple of hours and see what he's got. Then I'll wake you.'

'Okay,' said Kirsten, 'but one thing, you were a field operative once, weren't you? You were right here like me.'

'What makes you say that? You know I don't talk history.'

'You're in heels, tight skirt, and a blouse and you took him down like it's nothing.'

'That's just management defence courses. You take them when you start.'

Kirsten caught the wry smile and nodded. That was about as close to Anna as she had ever got, the woman who kept everyone at a distance. Even Richard, probably her most trusted colleague, was not close to her. Kirsten turned and made her way up the stairs that led to the upstairs bedrooms.

Out of the three that were upstairs, she took the one that didn't have mouse droppings in it and lay down on a mattress that seemed to have springs that were used to attack you rather than support and cushion your weight, but she was out within a minute.

Kirsten rarely dreamed but she had started to become fretful, tossing and turning. She saw a girl lying on the floor, her throat slashed. Then the man at the bottom of the sea. It was Peter Harborough's face but there was another man beside him, weights wrapped around his legs. She saw John Mitchell's face, reaching out, 'Help me,' he cried. 'Help me.' And then Anna Hunt's high heels were boring down on his head.

Kirsten woke up with a start. Daylight was coming through the window but she heard a voice from downstairs. It was Richard.

'She wants you now, Kirsten; wake up.'

Chapter 8

Kirsten had been asleep for three hours. Her body felt like it had been punched for all three of those. Rising from her makeshift bed, she was glad to be up, still slightly shaken from the dream she had.

'On my way. Get us a coffee, Richard,' she shouted back downstairs.

'Make your own. Still babysitting.' Kirsten descended the stairs and made her way into the kitchen where she found the kettle was already boiling. Anna was staring out of the window.

'Scared him good. He just kept writing, and writing, and writing. Most of it's nothing. Accurate, true. It's not a pile of crap. It's just not very entertaining, but there are some nuggets in it.'

'What sort of things?' asked Kirsten.

'Peter Harborough had a number of houses around the country. Whatever he was into, whoever he worked with, and Mitchell says he doesn't know, at times they needed to meet like we do. He had several places, or rather, his girlfriend did. They're all in her name, often hired out as holiday lets, but with a low uptake. According to Mitchell, Peter Harborough once boasted to him how he made it run. It looked like holiday lets because every now and again, he would do that. There was a woman in each of them who came in and cleaned every week, but he always had somewhere available.

'He never liked them to be booked all at the same time, so, there was usually two or three in the same part of the country. They made enough from them to keep them and pay off the mortgages. No doubt that's probably a boast. The other things he was getting involved in probably covered them, but what we have is a list of addresses. He's pretty sure that Peter used them to hide things and stash everything of use. It's time to go for a drive, Kirsten. It could be an extensive one. Come with me.'

Kirsten poured herself a coffee and followed Anna over to the dining room table where a map of Scotland was laid out. There were red circles in Aberdeen, Wick, a few on the west coast, near Lochinver down to Skye, Oban, a few in the borders, and one ring down near Stranraer.

'Like I said, he seems to have them all over. I know you're tired, Kirsten, but it's time to hit the road. Given where we are, probably best head over to Aberdeen and up round to north then down the west side. You can cut across Glasgow and Edinburgh if you wish, end up down in Stranraer, but make it quick.'

'You could send others out as well. That's an awful lot of houses to cover. What is there? Nearly ten, fourteen?'

'Now there are fourteen houses, but it's only you looking at them. I'm not sending anybody else out. I mean it. I'm keeping this quiet until I know where we're going and what we're finding. If word gets out about this, they could go in first to those houses before we even get near to them and take anything that's on that paper. There are accounts and other contacts that I can look at. I'll run the electronic side. The physical side, you're going to have to go and do.'

'You're not even going to trust Justin to do the computer side for you? He's good. You know he'd run that through in no time.'

'He could do, but like I say, I'm keeping it close. I don't trust Justin, not with this. Somebody comes up to the office, and he'll drop all of it. Do not tell him anything, for he'll drop it in conversation to have a good leer. You know what I'm talking about.'

Kirsten certainly did. She had always reckoned he was a sexist pig. Inside, she felt almost like a moral victory was being achieved, the man kept out of the main action because of this creepy defect he had.

'Here's your list of addresses,' said Anna, and handed Kirsten an A4 page. 'Careful what you send me as well,' said Anna. 'Careful how you send it. When we speak keep it in a code. Nothing overt. I'll ask you how your brother was working around that.'

Kirsten wasn't happy. Her brother was a sore subject. Looking at the addresses, she knew she wouldn't be seeing him for a couple of days, at least.

'Well, I best get on,' said Kirsten.

'You best had,' said Anna. 'Be thorough. If he's got a safe house, it's still not going to be out in the front and open. Anything that's been important, any information he's given if he's written it down, if he's kept it, it will be well stashed away. Don't bust any place up. We're on the quiet with this, so, stay quiet.'

Kirsten downed her coffee. It was hot and almost scalded

her throat, but it was good. She left her cup on the dining table and walked out. Outside, she looked around at an estate that had seen better days and made her way to her second car, the first now having no rear window. Then she drove off through Inverness on the road out to Aberdeen.

The morning was busy and the road to Aberdeen slow. Kirsten found herself constantly dipping her head as if she was about to fall asleep, but she kept alert as best she could, checking her mirrors, making sure no one was around her.

It took Kirsten a full day to check two houses in Aberdeen, another two in Wick, and then two located around Lochinver. She spent the night in her car, sleeping on the roadside for four hours. By lunchtime, she had checked a couple of houses on Skye on her merry way down to Oban for the next two. It took her the rest of that day to get across to Glasgow and Edinburgh, and then down to the border so that by the time she was heading towards Stranraer, the sun was coming up on another day. This was the third since she'd left the house in Inverness.

Kirsten wanted to change; she still had on the same clothes. She felt that she smelled, but she didn't have time for a break. She was also feeling a little down, guilty about not visiting her brother. Finally she arrived at the small village of Lendalfoot to investigate a little house at the side of the road. It was no more than a holiday cottage, barely three rooms. Its wide exterior looked out onto the sea and the crisp ocean air helped keep her awake.

She parked a distance away before returning on foot, looking around for the gap in the rather light traffic that was passing by before she nipped round to the back of the house. Taking out some picks, she unlocked the rear door, a job that was considerably easier than some of the other doors she had hacked through, as it was a simple turnkey lock. Sometimes that was the best way to do it. If you set up an elaborate security system, people would know something was inside, but this looked like a simple holiday home.

Opening the rear door, she entered the kitchen and started to examine every cupboard, taking out the pots and pans, the jars of coffee, tea bags that were left inside. The bright side was it was a holiday home, and therefore, there was not a lot of food kicking about. Kirsten did empty the coffee jar completely before pouring it back in. She checked the tea bags, feeling each and every one to see if there was anything hidden inside one of them. When she had thoroughly gone through the kitchen, she made her way into the front living room, lifting the sofa, checking underneath the cushions to see if there were any strips inside any of the seats.

She checked in and around the television. It was an old set but she managed to unscrew the rear casing and look inside it. There was nothing there. Every picture was turned over, the carpet lifted. Then when she made her way to the bedroom, she went through every piece of linen that was available until after an hour she sat down on the sofa in the living room.

This was the last house, and she had come up empty-handed. Anna wouldn't be happy, but then again, you could not find something that was not there. Even Anna couldn't do that. Kirsten let her shoulders drop. Right now, she could do with someone to rub her shoulders. It didn't have to be anybody handsome. It didn't have to be some strapping bloke. It just had to be somebody who knew what they were doing with muscles. She would lie there and they would beat her back, then work the magic across her blades and the top of her arms.

Maybe they could work on the legs as well. Maybe it would be good if they were good-looking as well. Kirsten had not had time for a boyfriend in so long. Even when she was working on the murder investigation team out of Inverness, she had no boyfriend. It did not seem weird then because neither had her boss, Hope McGrath, although she had heard on the grapevine that she had one now. It was good working for the undercover services, but it was also a lonely life. She couldn't talk to people about it and she was going out less and less.

No, the job was taking over more and more. That was the problem. When she was not working, she was training, desperate to keep up her mixed martial arts. She would flop into bed at night, exhausted, occasionally reading a book, something philosophical, but she rarely got past a chapter before it dropped onto the floor. Here she was, stuck in a little house in Lendalfoot, realizing that the glamour of it all was no glamour at all.

Kirsten laid her head back against the sofa to rest. Something caught her eye. There was a mark on the ceiling. It was thin, possibly a gap. She jumped up and sprinted to the wall.Above her was a hairline crack. The house had a roof space, but she had found no access to it within the house. There were no water tanks above, and she thought it must be a space to lock in the heat, a sloping roof that was there simply to run the rainwater away.

Kirsten made her way around the house again looking up, but no, there was no way to access up above. She saw no pipes up there. Maybe there were electrics, although, she couldn't see that either, but it wasn't uncommon for electrics to run above a roof through the ceiling. Depending on the slope, you did not always have a hatch to get up there.

Kirsten made her way back over to the hairline crack she had seen. Putting her hand up, she pressed at the roof. It didn't move. She pressed harder trying not to be overconfident and make a break in the ceiling. Slowly, a small piece of ceiling at the side of the hairline crack began to move upwards. It was extraordinarily heavy, and she was on tiptoe, standing on the edge of a seat to reach it. It took both hands to push it up, and then cast it aside. Kirsten moved to the kitchen to pull out a taller chair. Bringing it back, she reached up into the void with her hand.

Fumbling around, she found a tin and brought it down into the living room. She flicked it open but there was nothing inside. Slowly, Kirsten replaced everything and then sat down on the sofa again. Why have a secret hiding hole with nothing in it? This would certainly be a good place. Lendalfoot was out in the middle of nowhere. Yes, there was Stranraer to the south, but here was well clear of Glasgow and Edinburgh, any of the big cities. A person could be out here without anybody knowing, a simple place. It had struck Kirsten that some of these plans they had made would have been fairly recent.

It had only been a week or two since James Gunn had been approached so all plans must have been recent. Maybe what was in the tin had been recently destroyed. Kirsten thought about the kitchen. There were matches there, also a gas stove. Any of those could set fire to paper.

Taking a step outside the rear door, Kirsten saw the bin. There was one for recycling and on opening it, she couldn't see any paper inside. The other bin was reasonably full and stunk. Clearly, it hadn't been emptied. When was the last time that Peter Harborough had been here?

He had been trying to fix up a job. Had he real estate

here? Had he known? When the man had come for him at the jewellery store, he had been calm as if he was ready for it. Maybe he had known that things were going south, trying to play it better. Had he come out here to destroy any information? What was hidden in the roof? Had it been taken or had he destroyed it?

Kirsten pulled the bin inside the house, tipped it over, and slowly removed the rubbish onto the floor. She stunk already, so, this couldn't get any worse. A coke can was thrown this way. Remains of a packet of sausages joined it. There was a banana. Bit by bit, Kirsten separated out the rubbish until she had to scrape the side of the bin. It was there she found the remains of paper, burnt paper.

Taking a plastic bag from her pocket, she scraped off piece after piece. Placing the pieces inside the bag, most of it looked black, charred. After an hour of going through the bin, scraping off slowly what she could find, Kirsten replaced the rubbish, cleaned up the floor, and put the bin out at the rear. She then took the plastic bag through to the lounge, set it down on a table, and stared over it. Slowly, she began to remove each piece of paper.

Most were black and it was difficult not to let them break into smaller pieces. She carefully picked out those that still had white bits remaining, setting them down on the floor. As she worked her way through, it became apparent that most of the writing was destroyed. The man had done an excellent job of burning the paper. He had simply dumped the ashes into the bin, but Kirsten was able to pick out three bits of white paper, or at least white in the centre, for they were brown around the edge heading to black where they'd been properly burnt.

On one was written a word, and although the H was half

disappeared, Kirsten thought it said hit. There was a 1 with an S and what looked like the start of a T. 'The first,' thought Kirsten. But what was on the other piece of paper? It was the largest even though it was no bigger than her thumb. Most of the paper was brown, but there was a faint pencil writing over the top. It had all but gone, but as she stared, Kirsten could make out the words, 'Spear of destiny.'

The word hit was no big deal. They knew one was coming. First. First of what or where? Was it the first place or the first street? That wasn't of much use, but, spear of destiny, just what was that?

Chapter 9

Kirsten Stewart sat on the beach looking out into the waters of Loch Ryan. The ferry was making its way down to Cairnryan packed with tourists and commercial lorries on one of the main trade routes between Northern Ireland and Scotland. She saw the way the ferry broke through the water, leaving the wake at the back. Even in the cool air of an overcast sky, she felt somewhat at peace with the lapping waves. There was still a tiredness coursing through her body, her shoulders were tight and sore from all the driving she'd done. But now she had something to hold on to, something to chase after. Like the Whippet that's finally got the hare, she wasn't going to let go.

Sitting at a picnic table with a view out to choppy water, Kirsten had her laptop open in front of her, running through Google searches for the Spear of Destiny. She had no idea what it was. Was it a group? Was it an actual weapon? Was it a philosophy? Where did it come from? Who was it about? Some of the first searches that came up mentioned a fantastical spear, but she quickly realised that these were all fictional. There were several books written, again, novels with that title. She continued to scroll down. Soon the search broke into part answers, returns where the query wasn't repeated in the answer, Door of Destiny, Spear of Justice, things like that. She shook her head, took a deep breath, and continued to look through the results.

As she reached the bottom of her third search page, she saw a PDF from Glasgow University. Clicking on it, a political article was displayed talking about groups that sought to overthrow governments, destabilize regimes, and there, mentioned in the article, was the Spear of Destiny.

Kirsten read on. The Spear of Destiny was simply mentioned as an atypical group. There was no mention of the entity behind it, no mention of who started it. She scanned down into the citations and bibliography that followed, but there was no reference. Returning back to the top of the PDF, Kirsten saw the name, Dr. Chandra Smith. Her mind started racing. Who was this person? There was no photograph, but there was an attachment to the university, and so she decided that was where she needed to start. Googling up the university's number, she got in contact with the main switchboard and found that Dr. Smith was indeed available at the faculty. He may have been at lectures. The switch desk couldn't say, but they weren't able to contact him on his phone. Stewart thanked them, left the beach, got into her car, and drove to Glasgow.

Looking through some of the back-road scenery of the southwest of Scotland, Kirsten almost felt at home for a while. The driving was easy on the eyes although it felt a little slow due to the corners. She came upon a tractor and could not get past for half a mile. Her frustration built up as well, partly due to her was tiredness. She loved this part of the country as much as any other in Scotland. Anywhere out from the big city was good, and yet she wouldn't leave the city. She needed her gyms and her shops, places to browse, coffeehouses. In her heart, she was a city girl, who desperately wanted to be in the country.

The particular faculty of the university was on the west side of Glasgow, for which Kirsten was grateful, driving in from that side of the country. She routed to what looked like a development from the '70s, a concrete structure, four tall stories with much glasswork, but she thought very little spirit. Making her way in through the front door, she saw a receptionist glance at her. Kirsten reckoned she must have taken her for a student. Her baseball cap was on, a leather jacket over her shoulders, and the jeans probably topped it all off. That was fine.

Kirsten was okay with people thinking she was anyone but who she actually was. If things got tight, she could always pull her identification and get a way through to Dr. Chandra, but for now, she made her own way up, finding his political faculty on the third floor. Two left turns later, she stood outside a small door and knocked loudly. 'Just a moment,' came the reply.

The door opened and Kirsten saw a man she thought to be of Indian descent. He looked possibly to be in his forties, and behind him, the wall was awash with books. His desk had papers scattered here and there, and the room contained a very small table, at which stood two chairs, and there were a number of photographs on one of the other walls. Kirsten clocked the man receiving some sort of award in one of them.

'I've told you before, this is not the time for private discussion. I work today, but I am available tomorrow afternoon if you wish to speak then. What's your name, Miss?'

'Stewart. Kirsten Stewart, and I'm not one of your students, sir.'

'Then who the hell are you, and why are you here?'

'If we could just step inside, Dr. Smith. I need your assistance.'

'And I need to do some work. As I said, who are you?'

Kirsten reached down inside her leather jacket and pulled out her identification. The thing about her current identification was it didn't say who she really was, it just made some reference to being part of the police force. Most of the people in the service had come either from a police or military background, along with a few other specialists from other fields. 'It's government work, Dr. Smith. I need your time. My apologies for interrupting your work.'

Kirsten always felt it was good to be polite. She learned that from Macleod. Only when someone was being obstructive or bloody-minded, should you pull out the big guns, force your way through. Generally, with experts, if they felt they were needed, they divulged more information than you would get out of them simply by submitting a request.

'Well, come in then,' said Dr. Smith. 'I am quite busy. Take a seat and tell me what you need to know.'

Kirsten withdrew the seat that was offered, sitting beside the small desk that the doctor must have used for his tutorials. The man joined her but without any pleasantries. 'I'm investigating a group, Doctor, and I've run into some information about them. I need to know who they are.'

'Well, is there some sort of a name or something?' asked the doctor, clearly agitated that he was missing out on his own work.

'The Spear of Destiny, that's all I have, but I know you quoted it in one of your reports.

'Dissertation,' said the doctor, 'and I'm not sure you're correct. Spear of Destiny, it seems like a very remote topic. A little bit dramatic for some of the groups I write about. I'm much more into trade unions, and that sort of thing.'

'Believe me, you did write about them,' said Kirsten, and pulled out her phone, tapping keys and inputting into the Internet until she found the Google search result, bringing it up onscreen. She spun the phone around, presenting it to the doctor.

'That's a throwaway line, but I must have got it from somewhere,' he said. 'Just give me a moment. That paper is maybe three, four years old. It's not what I'm currently working on.' The man stood up and disappeared behind his main desk, and began pulling files out from the shelf behind him. Kirsten watched as he shook his head, flicking through this file then another. Then he began producing books off the shelf as well. After ten minutes, he had a large pile, and he was looking clearly embarrassed at the fact that he couldn't recall his own research.

'As I said, this must have been a throwaway line, something small. Please, just give me a moment. If you want tea or coffee, there's a machine down the hall. You can go and get it from there.'

Kirsten shook her head. She knew what it was like to trawl through detail and try and recall what you had seen before. She had a mind for it and Macleod had utilized her so often in that fashion.

'Ah,' said the doctor, 'I think I know where I saw them now. Just a second.' He spun round, knelt down, and pulled a couple of books from the very bottom shelf of his rather impressive library. He took a book, opened it, and started scanning it with his finger, muttering to himself.

'Chapter 7 . . . Chapter 7 . . . at the rear. That was it, at the rear. Let's see. Oh yes, this is it. Small fringe group. I'm surprised you don't have them in police records. But, in fairness, they didn't do much.'

'What did they do?' asked Kirsten.

'They were protesting. It was over a nuclear power station, as I believe. I think they're quoted in the article as being a failed group. One that never got off the ground, unable to take positive action. I actually spoke to one of their leaders on the phone.'

'Can you remember his name?'

'Not offhand, and he didn't give a full name. That was the other thing about them. They're quite secretive. He used some ridiculous name like Chucky or something. I think he heard my name and decided that would sound good alongside it.'

'What was their deal with the nuclear power station?'

'Well, they're an anti-weapons group. They didn't want nuclear power for anything. They see it as an evil. The power stations were looking to get renewed. This is from maybe ten years ago. They were putting in objections, but they were unable to galvanize any real momentum behind them. That's why they're in the article as a failed group. The other point I made was there was no notable figure. You see, you need a figurehead, someone that people can rally around. People don't look at groups. Lots of comic books and other stories talk about movements which don't have a figure. That's very rare. Even when the Berlin Wall came down, the figure was already there. It was the Berlin Wall itself, but for other groups, especially political, sometimes you need a figure to rally around. Well, it's like Britain rallying around Winston

78

Churchill in the war, that sort of dynamic leader. You don't necessarily have to be the brains behind the outfit, but they do need to be seen as driving ahead. People want to join a rolling maul, they don't want to join something that's stopped, so if you are not seen to at least be generating noise, people don't follow you. Spear of Destiny just fell flat on its face.'

'I take it the nuclear power station went ahead?'

'Yes, it was an updating extension of life, that sort of thing, and it sailed through without a problem. Despite reasonable arguments that they made, if you read the paperwork, it was fine, but nobody does. The arguments need to be made by a character. In a court of law, you have these barristers, and they're all dramatic, and waving arms, and stating things. It's not made by some sort of civil service grey figure.'

Technically, Kirsten Stewart was a civil servant, and for all the time she had been in the civil service, she certainly did not see dull and grey-figured people, but then again, she had not worked in the customer-facing units either. She did not consider the police a customer-facing unit. More like the cavalry.

'Would they be going by any other name?' asked Kirsten. 'I've done a search through the internet, and I can't come up with Spear of Destiny except in your article. You have a book that mentions them, and I didn't even bring that up in Amazon.'

'That's more of a technical book, not really the sort of thing that'd be bought by the mass market. One run goes out of print. It's only boring old farts, like me, stuck away in grey buildings like this, that read it.'

'You're not exactly old,' said Kirsten.

'If you're over twenty-five, every student here thinks you're old. I think I got away with polite comments because of my heritage. My father was British, but my mother was Indian, hence Chandra. Well, it's my first name, but Smith is my second. These days, you certainly don't offend the ethnics, do you?'

It struck Kirsten that if anybody else had said that, if they had not been from India or indeed from an ethnic background, that would have been offensive in itself. Sometimes, she found PC rules to be rather bizarre, but maybe they were better than some of the abuse that was given out before.

'Like I say, Dr. Smith, would you have any idea of any other names the group would go under? Any possible contacts?' The man delved back into the book he had produced from the bottom shelf. He didn't say a word but kept scanning the book, turning page after page. Then he stopped, lifted his head, and smiled at Kirsten Stewart.

'The Lamplight,' he said. 'They may be known as The Lamplight, but you probably won't find them on Google. Lamplight was their inner circle, it was an invited-persons-only group, the core that drove all the policies, who wanted to make all the difference. The Spear of Destiny was the outside persona that never took off, so, I'm afraid I can't direct you to a particular person. You may be more in a better field to find out if Lamplight still exists. I take it you're not ordinary police, are you?' asked the doctor.

'I am the police,' offered Kirsten, 'just a rather more special-ized division of it.' This was a lie. She was from the security services, but you never admitted that in front of anyone.

'Well, thank you for your time, Dr. Smith. I appreciate it, and if anybody else comes looking and asking, I wasn't here, and you don't know anything.'

'Like I said,' the man smiled, 'you're not normal police, are you? My mouth is sealed, my lips are shut. They won't get anything from me. Good luck, Ms. Stewart.' Kirsten grinned as she left the building and made her way down to the street outside. She was feeling peckish and asked a nearby student where she could get something to eat.

'Union is just there,' said the girl. 'Why don't you grab something in there? Well, you've got your card and that, haven't you?'

Kirsten grinned. When she started working a proper job, she always thought she would start to look older, not be seen as the fun person she was, but here she was, being misidentified as a student. She would contact Anna Hunt first though, reporting what she'd found, and ask Anna to put out a feel for any chatter about the Spear of Destiny group or about Lamplight. Until Anna came back, it was probably a good time to get some food and put her head down in the car. As she walked to the students' union, she laughed to herself.

Her former boss, Hope McGrath, had seen her in Inverness and asked her how the glamour life was going. Kirsten had told her when she had found it, she would come back to her.

Chapter 10

Kirsten could feel the mobile on her leg vibrating, causing her to mutter. As her eyes opened, a shaft of daylight blinded them and she shook her head trying to register what was going on. She was behind the wheel of her car, parked, and clearly, she had been asleep. Her memory flooded back to her grabbing a doze when Anna Hunt went off to find out information. Glancing at her watch, Kirsten realised that she had been asleep for nearly five hours. It wasn't a bad thing considering how much she had travelled recently, but it was now heading towards dinner time when people would be returning back from a day's work. She had a feeling hers was about to start.

'Yes, it's Kirsten,' said the bleary-eyed Stewart.

'You can answer the phone a bit quicker. It's not as if you're running around in the middle of life-threatening danger.' Anna Hunt's tone was sarcastic, but she then quickly changed her tone, getting down to business. 'It's taken me a while, but I had to do it on the quiet. I can only find one thing with *lamplight* attached to it. There's a conversation from Anita Anderson. She's a known villain, responsible for things like GBH, stealing, theft, burglary and she was on the phone to a colonel near Fort

William. There was a brief mention of *lamplight* and then a group called *Scotland's Trust.* They'd been in Fort William and Anita was keen to go. Much of the rest of the conversation was pretty mundane, you'd have thought they were talking about a national trust property or something, the way they spoke about the group, making action, getting things cleared from council, and things like this.

'There was definitely a group meeting in the area. The meeting was also that night, but that was four weeks ago. Apparently, it was a weekly meeting as described in the conversation. So, if I were you, I'd get hold of Anita Anderson. I've emailed you with a photo of her and her address. She lives just outside Fort William, so maybe get your skates on, and you might even be able to make the meeting. That's assuming she leaves from home. She doesn't currently have work, at least not any she's paying tax for. No car is registered, or with any known associates; neither is she looking for any dole money. She's obviously back to earning her money the good old way.'

'Any distinguishing features about her?' asked Kirsten.

'She's built like a brick house. She's over six foot and I wouldn't let her punch you.'

'Right, I'll get on it', said Kirsten. 'I'll try and let you know what I come up with.'

'Make sure you play it cool,' said Anna, 'don't rush in. I know I want results and I need them quick, but the last thing we need you to do is run in and blow your cover. We can't let them know we're on to them, whoever it is we are on to.'

'Understood. Play it cool. Find out what's going on. You know that could be another week before they have a second meeting?'

'Just play it how you see it. We brought you in because you

could get results. Macleod recommended you, said you were special. You realise Macleod doesn't say that about everybody?'

Kirsten hadn't. She knew he had recommended her, knew that he had encouraged her, told her that she was more than cut out for this, but she hadn't realised how vocal he had been. The Detective Inspector was never like that. Yes, he would be complimentary, but that statement seemed to be a little bit much for him. Maybe Anna Hunt was embellishing it. Either way, Kirsten wasn't going to leap too quickly. She would make her own judgment.

The drive out to Fort William was without incident. As the sun was setting, Kirsten pulled up at the address given to her by Anna Hunt for Anita Anderson. Reaching into her boot, she took out a box, quickly wrote out a label for Anita Anderson, and went to the door. After knocking on the door, there was a shout, and the door was opened. The woman before her was certainly not Anita Anderson. Kirsten Stewart was not bigger than many women, but she was bigger than this person. The woman was lucky to make five feet.

'Parcel for an Anita Anderson. Is she in?' asked Kirsten.

'No, she should be soon. Why? Just give it to me, I'll take it.'

'No, needs to be signed for, I'm sorry. When you say she's going to be back soon, do you know how long? I mean, I could probably pop around and do a few of the other deliveries and come back. Otherwise, I've got to come back out tomorrow. I'm not coming from here, I'm coming out from Glasgow.'

'Oh aye, what's in it?'

'Well, I don't know,' said Kirsten. 'I mean, I don't open them all and have a look.'

The woman paused to think. 'I'd say she'll be back in about five or ten minutes. If you come back then, you might get her.'

'I'll see,' said Kirsten. 'It depends how the other runs go. Don't tell her it's coming, I think it's meant to be a surprise.' The woman nodded, closed the door, and Kirsten went back to the car. She drove a little along the street, parked up and sat watching out of her rear-view mirror.

True to the woman's word, Anita Anderson arrived at the house five minutes later. The description of her from Anna Hunt sounded threatening but seeing the woman made Kirsten wonder if the term pulverizing fist was made for her. Her shoulders were wide, her legs like trunks, and yet she did not look to be out of shape. She had cropped blonde hair and wore a distinctive bomber jacket, red, with an eagle across the back.

Kirsten watched her enter the house and started wondering if she would disappear again tonight. The meetings happened every week, so she would have to tail her and just see what came.

It was an hour later when Anita Anderson, still dressed in her bomber jacket, exited the house, and began to walk. Kirsten got out of her car and tailed the woman from a distance, keeping an eye as the walk took her along the edges of Fort William and then into an estate with a community hall at its centre. Kirsten had ditched her badge and warrant card back in the car and produced a packet of cigarettes as she stood outside the community hall, smoking away. She had seen Anita Anderson go inside along with a number of other people, but rather than follow, Kirsten waited about twenty feet from the door and tried to look down and abject. There were more and more people coming by and one stopped.

'Are you okay?' asked the man. He was in his mid-twenties, dressed in a shabby T-shirt and jeans.

'Not really. It's all crap, isn't it?' said Kirsten. 'All rubbish.

Oh, I don't know what I'm going to do. Fed up, I am. Just fed up.'

'You on the streets?'

'Yes,' said, Kirsten. 'Not long here. Managed to get some bus fare and ended up here. Can't quite get to Glasgow yet. I can probably beg enough if I get to Glasgow. What's going on here anyway? There isn't somewhere warm in there, is there? Is that a meeting?' asked Kirsten.

'Yes. I don't know if you'll be interested though. The guy comes and he talks about Scottish history, I think he was in the army, but he's quite a challenge and he gives out free drinks at the end. You get some hot food sometimes. I started to come every week though you have to listen to some boring crap.'

'You say it's warm and there's food?' said Kirsten.

'Yes,' said the man. 'Afterwards, if you want, maybe you could come back and crash at mine. I've got a flat. Well, we've got a flat. There's a couple of us. Got somewhere warm if you want it though.'

Kirsten could see the man was eying her up, but he was a ticket into the hall. 'You look in pretty good nick though,' said the man. 'Have you been on the run long?'

'Left the woman's shelter. They're not bad there; they clothe you and that, but he was hanging around.'

'Who?' asked the man.

'Boyfriend, dealer, after me, so I had to run. I mean, they do their best to hide you, but—'

'I'll hide you, love. Not a problem. Come on.' The man bent down, put an arm around Kirsten's shoulder and encouraged her to stand. Kirsten let him drop the arm around her waist and she went into the hall with him, sitting down somewhere at the back. His arm didn't leave her waist. She leaned in, lying with her head on his chest, but her eyes were scanning everywhere. The people around seemed like the dregs of society to her, or was it the downbeats? She was unsure because some looked like drug addicts and others like people on hard times, but a few looked like activists, people who genuinely believed in the meeting they were coming to. There were no pamphlets, no flyers inside, but instead, a round of applause when a man stood up at the front of the hall on a small podium.

'Thank you all for coming. Tonight, we're going to talk about how this government has failed us. How you all are here looking for food and for a free meal. You see, brothers and sisters, I'm happy to feed you, but I want to give you more. You need to rise up with us.'

And so began the most banal forty minutes of speaking Kirsten Stewart had ever heard. The man wasn't inspirational, far from it. He did make a few good points about how divided society was. Just because she was a member of the services didn't mean that Kirsten didn't have her own opinions on how the country was run, but from the murmurs around her, she saw the people were not galvanized.

When the meeting had ended, Kirsten received a hot bowl of stew from her would-be hero. She pretended to like him, wrapping her arms around him several times, even giving him a peck on the cheek. The man was clearly becoming excited and once or twice he tried to force a kiss on her. Kirsten relented, then asked for selfies of him pretending she was falling for him. She spun this way and that way with him, camera high up in front of her taking the photos laughing away. All the while she was photographing the room, picture after picture, laughing like she was high on drugs. One thing she made certain of, was that she took plenty of photographs of the man who had spoken from the front.

'I think it's time we were heading back, love,' said the man. 'You still haven't told me your name.'

'Denise,' said Kirsten. 'I think you're right. Have you got a shower in your house?'

'Got a bath.'

'That'd be good enough.'

'If you're too tired, I could bathe you.'

'Sounds good,' said Kirsten, wrapped her arm around the man, and together they wandered out of the hall. Kirsten was bemused by the meeting in some ways. Yes, she could see why these people were there—there was a free meal. Some had even disappeared with alcohol, but there were very few that actually seemed interested in what was being said. She was sure there were drugs being dealt on the side. Maybe they were getting passed out for free as well.

So, what was the purpose of the meeting? She had lost Anita Anderson but at least she knew where she lived, and if required, she could always go back. If she did, she would have to wear a disguise so Anita's housemate would not recognize her as the woman who didn't deliver a parcel. As she walked along the streets of Fort William, the man steered her around to a back alley where he forcibly pressed Kirsten up against the wall. 'Can't wait 'til we get home, love,' he said, 'come on, let's get it on here.'

'Wait,' said Kirsten. 'Just wait a minute, I need to pee.'

'Not now, come on,' said the man. His hands ran down from Kirsten's shoulders towards her hips.

'I'll wet my pants,' she said. 'Just a moment, okay? I'm just going around the corner.'

Kirsten made it like she was stumbling, but when she turned

the corner, she picked up her pace and disappeared up the street, and made a right turn. She had left the alleyways behind and now began to run quickly, putting as much distance between Romeo and herself as possible.

What a lecherous creep, she thought. *Well, he certainly did me a favour.* Taking her phone out of her pocket, she started scanning through the photographs she had taken. At the time she wasn't sure how good they were, but she was able to see faces and plenty of them. *Time to see if my lucky dips worked*, she thought.

Returning to her car, Kirsten drove to a hotel chain and rented a room for the night. Inside, she made her way to the shower first, spending twenty minutes scrubbing the feeling of the creep off of her body. When she emerged, she had the towel set around her in front of the basic desk and mirror. She opened up her laptop and connected it securely to the agency's file system. There would be nothing untoward with her looking through faces; it was standard practice.

She input the faces for a match. Whether she did it or Anna Hunt did it, the record would be there, but there was no way she could sit all night going through faces herself, trying to find someone by pot luck in a crowd. Kirsten set the software off and running, pulled the faces off her mobile and sent them off to the servers that resided at head office. Once the process was running, she made her way over to the bed, lay down on it, and soon fell fast asleep.

Chapter 11

Kirsten awoke to find her laptop beeping. At first, she felt rather dazed looking around the room, then she reached out for her weapon that was kept just across from her on the bed. She came back to normalcy, sat up, stretched, and made her way over to the laptop sitting on the desk. A mirror behind the desk let her see her hair bedraggled and she thought about running a brush through it. Since she was sitting here with no one else, she decided that could wait until after a shower. The screen from the laptop lit up and Kirsten saw a number of results coming back from the photographs she had taken.

The computer had cross-matched them giving various degrees of accuracy and she knew she'd have to go through each result one by one. Fortunately, there were only ten. It took Kirsten five minutes to run through her photographs and the images given back by the computer to realise that only two of them were exact matches. Another one was dubious, a probable but not guaranteed, so Kirsten ignored it and looked instead at the two men now on her laptop screen.

One was a minor offender pulled in before for drugs, but the second interested her greatly. Alastair 'Jock' Murray had a round face and didn't look the picture of the master criminal. Instead, he was more like a jovial pirate with an earring hanging from his left ear. His bald head appeared to be suntanned in the photograph that was held as an image for him, and Kirsten glanced down at his record.

The man had a history of violence. He had served time for GBH and also aggravated assault, but there was nothing on him that tied him down to being part of a group that would actually go and kill people. But then again, a criminal record was just that, the things you got caught for.

Kirsten had been taught to be aware of the fact that many people did not have criminal records not because they were good, but simply because they never got caught. She looked down at the last known addresses for the man and realised the most recent was in Fort William, which tied up with him being at the meeting. She tried to recall what he was engaged in. There'd been so many faces that night and while she remembered him, he didn't stick out as doing anything memorable, usually being on the periphery of the meeting.

Kirsten closed her laptop, stood up, and made her way into the shower where she did some of her best thinking. Running a lather through her hair, she decided the best idea was to tail the man for a while, find out who he was, see if he could make introductions for the group.

Kirsten was well aware that she was running blind at the moment, trying against odds to fit into a secret group that clearly didn't want to be found, but possibly these other meetings were a front for it, a way of bringing people in. Maybe there was a political agenda in front of it. The meeting had certainly matched the previous efforts of the group to galvanize people.But when people weren't excited and when things weren't going their way, sometimes people took extreme action. It's often the minority that turned things around in a country. Often, a few individuals have changed the course of history.

Half an hour later, Kirsten was checking out of her room and taking the car into the heart of Fort William. The address for Alastair Murray was a top floor flat, and rather than make her way up, Kirsten sat in the street outside watching for signs of life from the building. It was after mid-day when curtains were opened and she saw a bald head. It was another hour before the man left his flat, walking into town.

Kirsten followed him, keeping her distance as ever, not wanting to get too close. Today, she wore an old baseball hat. Striding along in her t-shirt, jumper, and black leggings, she tried to appear as different as possible from the girl she was the night before.

The man entered a small café in the centre of the town.It was clean without being overly modern. Kirsten walked past the coffee shop to buy a paper before she entered the café and sat in the far corner. The man had ordered a coffee and three rounds of toast and did not seem to be looking for anyone else. Kirsten had a coffee herself and was intrigued to see a man enter who she had seen the night before. It was the colonel who had made a speech.He made a beeline for Alastair Murray, sitting down quickly in front of him and placing a number of posters on the table, dropping one on the floor before sweeping it back up. With a quick glance, Kirsten read them upside down and realised they were calls for the rally that had taken place the night before. Clearly, it was a weekly event.

Fortunately, the café was fairly empty. Only the odd noise of cleaning dishes and the water boiling prevented Kirsten from overhearing the conversation fully.

'You'll be on the door again next week, Jock,' said the colonel. 'I didn't see anyone last night. Did you find anyone?'

'No. You're doing the wrong thing with this, you realise that. You're not going to get anyone of quality walking in. You're going to need someone who can handle themselves, that's what she said. Someone that is in control, not panic, but a true believer. Someone there for the cause.'

'And preferably a woman too. He likes his women. That's what she told me and she wants to keep him as happy as possible, at least until he gets his job done. No hiccups, nothing that can go astray. This is important, Jock, we need to pick the right one.'

'But I told you last night there wasn't anyone.'

'Time's running short, she needs someone, and she needs them soon.'

'What do you want me to do? Just magic someone out of thin air. I can grab you any Tom, Dick, or Harry off the street.'

'Don't get touchy. You know I know the trouble you're having with it. Could be time now to maybe think about something else, hiring somebody in.'

'No,' said Jock. 'You hire someone in, you know the problems that come with that. They've got connections. We need somebody who's no one. Someone who can just disappear. We'll pick him up coming through the airport, you know that. They'll be on to him, then they'll be onto them. So, we need somebody who can disappear afterwards.'

'Well, we've only got another couple of meetings, so you better find someone soon,' said the colonel, 'but I'll leave that in your hands. I've got enough other planning to do here as the post is for three days' time.'

Stewart ordered another coffee as the colonel left. As he cast a glance at the man, he began to shake his head. The man then abruptly stood up, shoved his chair under the table, and left a small number of coins, presumably to cover his food.

Kirsten made her way out onto the street after him. He was a good thirty yards ahead on the far side of the street when she exited. She crossed over, keeping her distance and watched the man walk out of town where he seemed to be striding up towards the canal that sat high above Fort William. She had once run an investigation up there when she was back on the murder team, an incident that was now commemorated by a plaque at the side of the canal where German tourists had died.

Kirsten remembered the gory scenes she had arrived at. As with all things, horror was replaced with beauty and aside from the plaque, you wouldn't have known what had occurred. She watched the bald-headed man clamber up beside Neptune steps, the large number of locks that take boats up from the sea at Corpach, up to the Caledonian canal that eventually ran into Loch Ness and on to Inverness.

Kirsten was able to race around the man and position herself up ahead of him, hoping he was going to walk further on along the canal. When he was barely in sight, she placed herself at the side of the canal, throwing her shoes behind her into a hedge. She took her socks off as well, and dirtied her feet, shaking her hair out. She took some grass, rubbed it through her hair before lying down as if asleep.

When Alastair Murray approached, Kirsten made a jump, as if she had a shock, and then stared up into the eyes of the man looking down at her. 'You haven't come for me, have you?' she

94

said.

'Easy, love. What are you doing down there?'

Kirsten stared at the man, then a sudden look of realization swept across her face. 'Is it you?' she said.

'I think you must be dreaming about somebody from home, love,' said the man, and went to turn away.

'No, it is. The meeting last night. You were at it, weren't you?'

'Which meeting would that be?' said Jock.

'The one we got the food at. The guy who stood at the front, Colonel someone, he called himself. Made a lot of sense to me, made a lot of sense. I'm on the rough end, you see. Can you see that?' I hear nothing good for me. You're right about this country. You're right about this place. It's all for those at the top. Not friendly to the rest of us, is it?'

The man bent down. 'That's true, isn't it, love? Not for us at all. That's what he was saying, wasn't it? Who are you now then? What's your name?'

'Jennifer. You can call me Jen if you want. Not all my friends do. Well, not all my friends did. They're not about anymore, are they?'

'Why are you here, Jen, by the side of the canal?'

'Easier to sleep up here. You don't get police coming after you if you're not in the doorways to shops. Sleep up in a hedge up here. If you're lucky, you might find food leftover in the bins from the tourists, people on the boats. Sometimes if you're lucky you can run onto a boat and pinch stuff. You don't believe what people do on boats.'

'What? You're just some scraggy runt?'

'Don't take that tone with me,' said Kirsten. 'I had a proper job until they got rid of me. Until we got fired, all closed down.

Kicked out, struggled on the dole, kicked me out of the flat. I didn't have any rich, posh parents to look after me. No, they just said I was trouble. Trouble because of the childhood I had. My fault, I didn't have parents. Foster home here, foster home there. Some of them don't really care about you, do they?'

Kirsten could see the man was beginning to get interested and he reached forward with his hand. 'Let me help you up, love. Why don't we go for a walk?'

'I don't do that, all right? I'm not just some scraggy runt. I'm not looking to give you a blow job or something to get some money. I saw you at the meeting, that's the whole thing. It's the meeting. I recognized you from the meeting. He said I could do something. The Colonel guy said we can change things. I need somebody to help me change things. It's hard to change things when you're down here. It's all right for you guys wandering around, but you've got a nice car and a flat, the same with Colonel. The rest of us down here, we got nothing.'

'I wasn't looking for anything, love. I just thought you should come. Why don't I buy you something, a coffee and then we can have a little chat about you? Nothing more, nothing less, okay? Get you some food, so you don't have to nick anything out of the bins. I might even buy you a pair of shoes as well.'

'All right, then. But I mean it when I say there's nothing else.'

The man laughed, reached down with his hand, and pulled Kirsten to her feet. Together, they walked back into town, mainly in silence until they reached a small café, thankfully, a different one to which the man had been in before. Maybe that was because that was where he met the colonel and he didn't want somebody hanging around and interfering with their discussions. Certainly, the woman who then brought them food didn't recognize Alastair Murray.

Kirsten greedily ate through a plate of mince despite the fact she wasn't hungry at all.

'You haven't eaten in a while. Have you?'

'I got enough. I told you how I got it. Just, this is nice, isn't it? Nice to get something proper for a change.'

'You're interested then in coming to the group, are you? Interested in helping out.'

'I didn't say that. You might find I'm not in the best situation to help out, am I?'

'No, it seems like you're not, but if you want to come along and help out, if you can be good for us, maybe be we could give you a bit of accommodation, somewhere to sleep, set you up.'

'Really? You could do something like that. This isn't just some scam? You don't people traffic or that, is it?'

'You're not daft, are you? You are always on the lookout for the bad thing. That's good. Got your wits about you.'

'Well, you have to, don't you?' said Kirsten. 'Plenty of people about like that. That's what's wrong with our society. We don't deal with them, don't sort things out. Colonel said he would sort things out. But you're not getting really far, are you? Most of the people there were there just for the food.'

'And you weren't?' said the man.

'Yes, I was, at first, but I hadn't heard him, had I? I hadn't heard what he had to say. Mind you, he's not the most enigmatic speaker, is he?'

'Enigmatic? You have had an education, haven't you?'

'I told you,' said Kirsten, 'I wasn't always like this, so what's the deal? You going to help me or not? If you're not, I need to get back up there and start begging for my next meal.'

'Tonight,' said the man, 'the field behind where I met you.

Be there, midnight.'

'Midnight? What do you think this is?'

'Midnight,' said the man. 'I need you to go and meet somebody special. You only saw the front-end of what we do; well, we try and cause a little bit of mischief for this government. That means that we need to be discreet when we go places.'

'What sort of mischief?' asked Kirsten.

'Nothing sinister. Posters up over their headquarters, things like that. Nothing too illegal, but stuff you don't want to get caught for. They use any excuse to put people down.'

'At midnight? Okay. Will go for it, but you better be good, man. I mean, this is all just a little bit dodgy, isn't it? I'll keep my wits about me.'

'Okay. What are you doing for the rest of the day though?' he asked.

'I'm going to go up there and sit down like I normally do and see if I can get some more money in case your thing's a bust tonight.'

'Don't worry, love,' he said. 'It's not a bust, it's genuine. I don't like to see a gal on hard times, especially, one who's got so much to offer, especially, when she looks after herself. You've no idea how many will turn around and try to bed me to get their food and somewhere to sleep.'

'Well, some of them are not as clever as me, are they? It's not their fault.'

'No, it isn't,' said the man, 'but maybe you can help us change that. Tonight, midnight, in the field.'

Kirsten watched the man put money down on the table and then walk out. The woman behind the counter was quick coming over and taking it off the table and giving Kirsten a scowl. She had come in with bare feet after all. Kirsten was getting the feeling that she needed to move quickly or else the woman would throw her out. The man was watching at the window and Kirsten stared back at him. If he was any good, he would be watching her from here on. It looked like today was going to be a day of begging up at the canal.

Chapter 12

Kirsten spent the day sitting out by the canal. At some point, she knew she would need to hide her phone and ID, and other telltale bits on her. She was well aware that she might be searched. It was three in the afternoon when she spotted Alastair Murray on the other side of the canal. He was hiding in a bush watching her, binoculars up. Kirsten made sure she paid no heed to where he was.

Around half past four, Kirsten got up, made her way along the canal side, and jumped on board one of the boats. She came back off with a loaf of bread, hiding it until she got back into her begging place before removing it to eat. *That should satisfy him*, she thought. Shortly after that, Kirsten saw him disappear.

By seven o'clock, when the light began to fade, she pulled her shoes back out of the hedge, put them on and made her way back to the car by a circuitous route. Once inside the vehicle, she drove to the edge of town and placed a call to her boss.

Anna wasn't there, but her bodyguard Richard took a message. Despite Richard being a trusted individual, Kirsten remembered Anna's words so all she decided to say was, 'Contact going deep.' Anna would know not to expect a call for a while. Kirsten reckoned her boss would be pleased that she was delving into the investigation. Kirsten then parked the car at the edge of Fort William, took everything that she had inside her jacket pockets, leaving them inside before locking the car. She placed the keys inside a little plastic bag along with her ID.

Kirsten counted three traffic lights along, walked across to find a hedge, and dug into the ground to bury the plastic bag. She had left her shoes in the car as well, and by the time she got to the field she was sore due to the small cuts across the soles of her feet.

Kirsten reached the field by ten o'clock and found a hiding place where she could survey anyone coming towards it. There was a good line of sight to the path by the canal, but there was also another route up, a road that led through to a gate at the far end of the field. As she sat waiting, Kirsten felt her nerves beginning to jangle inside her. She was going dark and wouldn't be able to contact anyone, but she was going to find out exactly what these people were like. So far, they seemed a pretty amateur outfit.

Maybe she had the wrong group, posters or not, but the overheard conversation implied they were looking for someone for a job, a good-looking woman to pick a guy up. It was a definite possibility, and there was an excitement that she might get direct contact with this hit man, but also the fear that if she betrayed herself to them, it could also be the end of her. There was no backup this time. No call she could make. After all, she had left her phone behind as well.

It was midnight when the gate at the bottom end of the field opened and a Land Rover drove in. Alastair Murray stepped out and started looking around so Kirsten made her way from the hedge, walking over steadily, looking around her the whole time.

'Just you, is it?'

'Yes, Jen. It's just me. I'm going to take you to see someone.'

'Okay, where are they?'

'I can't tell you that, and I'm going have to get you to wear this black hood.'

'Oh, hey,' said Kirsten, 'easy; what's this all about?'

'I told you before, Jen, we do some things the government don't like, so we need to be okay, you know? We need to be covered, you can't just bring anyone in, for all I know you could be a plant.'

'A what? Look, man, I could go back up there and just hole up again. I mean, I can look after myself.'

'Yes, I heard. Now you in or not?'

'You haven't come through on anything though, have you?' said Kirsten. 'You took me for a meal; you said you'll come here and do this. All I know is I'm getting in with someone who's going to take me off and use me somewhere. Probably going to ask me to handcuff myself next.'

'No, but I did come through with something.' The man brought a bag out from behind his back and threw it towards Kirsten. She opened them up to find a pair of trainers.

'How did you know my size?' she asked.

'I didn't; you can tell me if they fit or not. I mean we can get you another pair, but come on, we need to get going. The person we're going to see doesn't hang about.'

'Is it that colonel guy?' asked Kirsten.

'No, it's not the colonel. The colonel is just the guy that talks. We're going to see the real boss.'

Kirsten tried on the trainers, walking around in them as if she was measuring them for size. 'Okay then, these don't feel bad; you may be half a size out, maybe a whole one.'

'It's better than walking around on your bare feet.'

With that, Kirsten turned, marched to the far side of the Land Rover, and got in. Alastair Murray sat beside her. 'So how do you do this, Mister?'

'It's Jock, okay? You can call me Jock. Everyone calls me Jock.'

'Jock, in Scotland?'

'All right, that's an old military thing.' The man offered no more. Kirsten sat back and the man produced a hood, placing it over her head. 'Okay, just sit there and don't take it off, don't try and look; otherwise, I'll just have to drag you back here and let you go. We're not big fry, but what we do can get us into trouble so I need to have people I can trust.'

Kirsten sat, her hands shaking slightly, trying to give the impression she was nervous. It wasn't difficult to do because she was anxious, but for different reasons. Kirsten reckoned they must have driven for twenty to thirty minutes but without a watch, she couldn't be sure when she arrived. As soon as the vehicles halted with its engines running, the hood was removed from her head.

'See,' said Jock, 'I'm not trying to do anything untoward here.'

Kirsten looked at the farmhouse in front of her. There were a couple of lights on within the main building, but a barn beyond it was fully lit with the door open. Jock continued to drive, taking the vehicle inside to park it.

'Get out,' said Jock, 'time to meet someone.'

Kirsten opened the car door and realised that the barn door behind her had been shut. There were a number of bales of straw sitting around and Jock pointed over to one.

'Sit there, I'll tell her you're here.'

'Her?' queried Kirsten.

'Yes, Jen. It's not a male chauvinist organization you're in at the moment.'

Kirsten sat down on the bale of straw and looked around. The barn was simple, and probably was in daily use. There was a tractor at one end, clearly put away so it wouldn't suffer any of the outdoor rigors. Kirsten felt for a while that she may have got the wrong place. Everything seemed very rustic. Was this a group of amateurs she'd stumbled upon? Was she about to get asked to do an illegal poster run along with some city hall or a council office wall?

Kirsten jumped up when she saw a man walk in. He had dark hair that reached beyond his shoulders. He had a weapon in his hand. It was a simple gun, but it did have a silencer on it. Jock followed him behind.

'What the heck's this?' said Kirsten. 'When did we start pulling guns?'

A woman followed Jock in and immediately held up her hands. 'Easy,' she said, 'that's just my protection. You'd be surprised who comes after us.'

'What do you need protection for?' asked Kirsten. She started looking around her, pretending to be nervous. Her hands grabbed each other, rubbing furiously. 'What the hell have you got me into, Jock?'

'Easy,' said Jock, 'you said you wanted to help, and you're smart, so stay smart. Just relax.'

The thirty-something looking woman came over to sit beside Kirsten. She wore designer jeans, long black boots, and had a blonde run of hair that went down past her shoulder blades to touch the middle of her back. She had one eye that seemed slightly lazy, not coming round to look fully at Kirsten.

'It's rude to stare,' said the woman, 'but it's my little thing. Got it during a protest, hit in the side with a gun, but then we do what we do for the cause, don't we?' Kirsten looked at her and continued to give the appearance of a nervous girl. 'Jock says you want in—you want to be part of this.'

'I'm not even sure what this is.'

'This is food for your belly. This is a place to stay. This is clothes, and a sweet lifestyle again. This is a chance to get back at those people that took everything away from you. That's what this is, but you've also come in, so you can't go out. You do realise that, don't you?' Kirsten was intrigued but she tried to give the look of terror across her face.

'What the hell? You can't just keep me here like this. I can walk out of here if I want.' Kirsten watched the man with the long black hair lift his gun and point it towards her.

'No, you've seen me,' said the woman, 'and I need to know that you're in with us, because you're either in with us or you leave that door in a bag.'

Kirsten looked over towards Jock. 'You said you were a small fry. You said we were doing posters and things. What the hell is it with the guns?'

'Just settle,' said Jock. 'You'll be fine. It's just a driving job for you. Just a driving job and we'll get you a flat.'

'A flat of your own. All you have got to do is be a gofer, drive me about, drive someone else about, that's all, we don't ask anything else. Maybe drop a few packages here and there. You understand, Jen, because you're a nobody, are you? Nobody knows where you are. I need someone. I need someone who is a nobody, someone who can get on with it. Someone I can make a somebody.' The woman reached inside her jeans pocket and pulled out a roll of notes, 'There's three hundred there,' she said. 'That's the down payment, but you've got to do your bit first.'

Kirsten didn't like the sound of this. She looked around the barn and thought, *there's nowhere to run, nowhere to hide.*

'Bring her in,' shouted the woman. Kirsten stared in horror as from the far door of the barn a young Asian woman was dragged in by the hair.

'People like this have come over; they've taken most of our stuff, all the benefits. You see them rising up. They're not true children of Scotland, are they? This government, they want equal rights for everyone; their agendas promote people like this. All PC these days, aren't we? These scavenging bastards come in and take stuff. I'm not happy about that, Jen. Do you know that? I'm not.

'This is one here though, she came through and got a free university degree and she didn't have to pay for it. Deemed to be in need while all our brothers and sisters sit in squalor, drugged up, drinking themselves silly while money goes to filth like this. You get that, don't you Jen? You were begging on the street and she was lapping it up. Time for consequences though, isn't it?'

Kirsten began to shake. She had a dread of what was coming. She knew they would want her to prove herself, but surely not like this. The man with the long black hair walked over to Kirsten.

'Come with me,' he said, and when Kirsten didn't move, he pointed the gun at her. She stood up, walked across to the centre of the barn. The man stood behind Kirsten, holding his gun towards her back. The blonde-haired woman then stood up and made her way across to Kirsten.

'I have a gun here,' she said, 'and I want you to take it, and I

106

want you to blow the brains out of this parasite.' The woman grabbed the Asian woman and pulled her down by the hair to her knees. She then struck her with the back of her hand. 'There you go, she's pruned for you. She might cry, she might make a whimper, but she won't hurt you. All you've got to do is pull the trigger.'

Kirsten felt the gun being thrust into her hand, but she felt the one with the silencer still in her back. How would she get out of this? Before her, the Asian woman was crying, choking with her own tears.

'Please. No. Don't.' Then came words in a language Kirsten didn't understand. Kirsten took the gun, held it against the back of the Asian woman's head. She could not turn quick enough to shoot the man behind her. There was no way out of this, but there was no way she was going to kill an innocent woman either.

Chapter 13

Kirsten could feel her hands shaking, the muzzle of the gun vibrating against the Asian woman's head. The woman fell forward several times, crying into the floor, her hands cuffed behind her back. Each time, the blonde-haired woman would pull her back up.

'Go on then. Show us you're part of us. Dispatch this filth.'

Kirsten's head swam. She thought about all the gruesome sights she'd seen in her time as a detective, all the violence and anger done to other people. She had never perpetrated something like this. Sure, she had been in fights, but this was just cold-blooded murder. What could she do? This was over the line, and yet she had a gun on her back. She too would be dead, and these people would just carry on. *Think, Kirsten, come on. You're the clever one. Macleod put you here for these situations. He said that you were the one, you were the one with the ability. You had the mind for this.*

'Do it!' said the blonde-haired woman. 'Do it now. I'll count to three if it helps. I'll count to three and if you haven't done it, I'll get my friend behind you to shoot you. If I reach five, you're dead. One, two.'

'Wait,' said Kirsten.

'There's no waiting. Three.'

'I said, wait. I can't pull this trigger. It's too risky.'

'Go on,' said the blonde-haired woman.

'We're not far away. The town's close to us. We're not that far out of Fort William. When I looked around, yes, I saw the barn, and I saw the house with its lights on. We're not so far in the countryside that a shot with an unsilenced muzzle isn't going to resonate everywhere.'

'We'll be out of here quickly,' said the woman.

'I'm not aware whose place this is. But this is your payday and you don't want to give that away. If you really wanted to kill her, why blow her brains out with a gun with no muzzle on it? Simply take a knife, slit her throat, drop her in some other way.'

'Good,' said the woman. 'You think. You just don't want to do what you have to do under pressure. A lot of people would have just pulled that trigger, and that would have pissed me off because she would have been dead. It's not that I care for her, but she's merchandise. I can make money out of her. Then I would have had to kill you as well, because you would've stood there and said I incited you. I brought you here. I couldn't trust that. I couldn't trust you with that, could I? No. I'd have had to kill you as well. You're smart, Jen. Very smart. Not afraid to call it as you see it. That's good. That's your first test. I'll see you again.'

With that the blonde-haired woman walked out of the barn and Kirsten caught a view of Jock giving a big whistle.

'My, you know how to cut it close. I thought you were a goner, Jen. I thought you were not as smart as you look.' Kirsten felt the gun being removed from her back, and the black-haired man stepped down in front of her, picked the

109

Asian woman up by the hair, forced her to her feet, and then dragged her out of the barn.

'What now?' asked Kirsten.

'Now we go back. You did well, but there'll be more tests. We don't just let anybody in like that.'

'How long until the flat, and the clothes, and all the rest of it?'

'Not long,' said Jock, 'but enough talking. In the Land Rover, I'll let you put your own hood on. We'll get back, but you did well in the distancing. We're barely outside of Fort William at all.'

Kirsten made her way over to the Land Rover, climbed inside the passenger seat, and pulled down the hood over her head. She heard Jock getting in beside her, starting the engine, and then driving off.

'Jock, just one more question.'

'As long as it's not, 'Who is she?' I guess I'll try and answer it.'

'What would she have done if I'd pulled the trigger? I know she said she would have killed me, but the shot would have rung out. It would have exposed the barn and everything.'

'That's why the gun wasn't loaded, but you might not have got much time to recognize that. I think the man behind you would have dispatched you.'

'Not the most pleasant of people, are they?'

'That's my boss you're talking about,' said Jock. 'You don't comment about her to anyone. You don't know who's close to her, really close.'

'But you said this is a political cause.'

'Of course, it is,' said Jock, 'but you've got to fund these things, haven't you? I mean, what's the problem with a few

Asian women working the game for us, eh? Wouldn't let a nice white girl like you go through that though. I reckon you could be a cut above this thing, Jen. You do the next couple of things right and you'll be marching around in a smart suit. You could get close to her.'

'I'll be happy doing the posters and that, you know that.'

'She wants some sort of driver, that's what I know. At least that's what I can tell you. That's what you're heading to be, so don't refuse it if she gives you it. She doesn't like people going off on their own game. Doesn't trust them, and trust can be a bit deadly.'

'Cheers, Jock,' said Kirsten. 'Where are you dropping me?'

'Why don't you crash at mine?' said Jock.

'I told you before, I'm not that sort of girl.'

Kirsten felt the hood being taken off her head. She looked around and realised they were inside Fort William now. 'Well,' said Jock, 'you probably guessed roughly whereabouts we were anyway, so not to worry. I'm not offering that; I'm just offering you a couch. You can have a shower and that if you want. I'll even let you lock the door.'

Kirsten watched him laugh and felt he was warming to her. She decided to play along. 'I haven't done this sort of thing before, Jock. You need to keep me straight. I can see if I offend someone, it's not going to end well.'

'Good. You've got a smart head on. I'll keep you straight, don't worry. You stick close to Jock, Jock'll sort you out.'

The Land Rover was parked on the far side of Fort William from Jock's flat, but from there they walked, Kirsten much more comfortable now in her new trainers. There was part of her that was running on momentum but inside, she knew there was a payback coming. She would have to wait for the right time to let it out. Kirsten had been seconds from having to blow the brains out of someone she didn't know. Either that or have her own brains being blown out. It didn't matter that the gun probably wasn't loaded, she still might have pulled the trigger. It would've been her doing it, and if they killed her, they probably would have killed the Asian woman for having seen her. Kirsten didn't buy the fact that a kept woman like that was merchandise they didn't want to damage.

As they reached Jock's flat, they made their way up the many steps until they got to a door at the top with a simple number ten on it. After unlocking the door, Jock flicked on a switch, and the room ahead lit up. The place was neat enough, a couch with a large telly, and in the background, a table with some models on it. Airfix models. Her brother used to build those when he was younger. There was also a large whisky cabinet, and Kirsten stood waiting to see where she was allowed to go within the room. Jock padded through to the kitchen, and Kirsten could hear the kettle going on before he came back in.

'Make yourself at home. Bathroom's through there. Have a shower now if you want. I'll have a cuppa for you when you come out, and then I'm off to bed. You can have the couch there. I haven't got anything for you to wear but you can sleep in your clothes or whatever you want. I won't be through till mid-morning, and you'll have the duvet and stuff, so what I'm trying to say is, Jen, don't worry about me. I'm not the guy who's going to do that with you, okay?'

Kirsten was struggling with Jock. In some ways, he was quite a questionable character. Yet he almost seemed to be caring for her, despite his involvement with such a nefarious gang of people. He almost stood and watched her shoot someone. Was he simply mixed up in something bad he couldn't get out of?

The man had been in jail for GBH and other violent crimes.

The hour was late, and Kirsten's head was spinning. She thanked Jock, made her way through to the bathroom, locked the door, and then stood for a moment. She felt the tears about to come, felt herself about to break down, so quickly, she turned on the shower, stripped off and climbed inside before sitting on the shower tray floor, letting all the terror that she had experienced when holding the gun to the woman's head come out. Tears flowed, but she fought hard not to sniff. Kirsten didn't want Jock to hear.

'Are you all right, Jen? Are you okay, love?'

'Yes,' said Kirsten, 'I'm fine.'

'You don't sound fine. It's all right. I got a stiff drink for you when you come out.'

It was twenty minutes before Kirsten emerged from the shower. She wrapped a large towel around her and another around her head, tying up her hair behind. When she opened the bathroom door, she saw Jock in the living room looking towards her, deeply concerned.

'Can take a lot out of people, especially if you're not used to that sort of thing. Come on over here, sit down.' Jock indicated the sofa, and Kirsten padded her way over.

'Do you mind if I wash my clothes?' said Kirsten. 'It's just, they obviously stink a bit.' Jock nodded and sat down beside Kirsten on the sofa. Before her on the table was a large whisky. As she laid back with it, sinking into what turned out to be a very soft sofa, Jock leaned in towards her.

'You've done good. It's going to be a shock, but you'll come out of the other side. I think you did good, girl.'

Kirsten looked up at him, and Jock's eyes were wide. Did he actually feel something for her, and was she something to be played on? She could not be too quick to play along with it. After all, she had been the girl who did not want anything, the girl who did not do anything, she wasn't that sort of girl. Therefore, she had to be careful.

'That wasn't easy, Jock,' said Kirsten, leaning into the man. 'It'd be nice to have somebody guide me through this.' Jock's left hand moved out and settled on Kirsten's knee. She could feel it start to rub up and down the lower end of her thigh.

'Just give it time and get that down you.'

Together, they sat in silence, Jock continuing to rub Kirsten's thigh, and she wondered how much he would try for, but she was deeply surprised. After a couple of minutes, he stood up. 'That is bedtime. I'll go get you some pillows and a duvet and you get yourself some sleep. I guess we'll find out in the morning just how much she thought of you.'

'You don't think I'm in any trouble?' said Kirsten. 'I mean, she did let me go there, didn't she? She would've done something if she thought I was a risk or something.'

'Yes, she would, but on the other hand, if I'm honest,' said Jock, 'you've seen her, so let's hope she does like you. Anyway, I'll get those pillows.'

Kirsten struggled to sleep that night, half wondering if this was a ploy. Would Jock come through, put a pillow over her and finish her off? On the other hand, the man seemed to genuinely like her. As creepy as it was that he ran his hand up and down her thigh while sitting in only a towel, she wondered how best to play this. When she had taken her training honey traps were thoroughly gone through; both how to avoid them and also how to play them. Not that she was ever offering her body up to be used in that fashion, but there was a way to flirt without giving anything away. A deep kiss, maybe even

114

a fumble, short of going to bed. If the role demanded it, the service would expect you to play it. Kirsten was comfortable with that bit. Any further was not for her.

In the morning, she awoke to the smell of bacon. When she toddled through to the kitchen, duvet wrapped around her, Jock presented her a pile of her clothes already washed.

'Did them for you,' he said. 'Hope they're okay.'

More like checked through my pockets, Kirsten thought to herself, *but he won't find anything, and that's good*. She sat down at the table, eating a fried egg with her bacon. The telephone rang and Jock picked it up.

'That's quick. Needed that quick, though. Okay. Yes. We'll get her over. I'll drop her in. On her own? Really?'

Kirsten watched Jock put the phone down, looking evidently disappointed.

'She wants to see you today. On your own, though, so you'd better have your wits about you. I'll tell you where you're going and you can get a bus out. Just be careful, little one. Make sure you know exactly what she wants from you and do it. Then you should be all right. Might even see you back here tonight. Jock'll look after you.'

Kirsten nodded, stood up in her duvet, toddled over, and placed a kiss on Jock's cheek.

'Thank you. I don't think I'd have been all right without you. I'll repay you one day. You'll see.'

This seemed to bring a smile to Jock's face, and Kirsten understood what sort of repayment he thought he was about to get. Making her way back to the front living room, Kirsten dressed quickly, quick enough to ensure that she had underwear on by the time Jock made his way into the room. He stood in the corner, watching her rush to get her clothes on, before coming over with a piece of paper and an address on it.

'You get the bus out of town. It should drop you maybe a quarter of a mile away. You'll have to walk the rest, but hey, don't get a taxi. She doesn't like that. Taxi drivers know where they've dropped you, bus drivers are just going to a stop.'

'Yes, that's understood. I guess you shouldn't wait up for me.' Kirsten smiled.

'Don't you worry. I'll be here waiting for you,' said Jock. With that, he reached forward, enveloping Kirsten in an embrace. She tilted her head back and allowed him to kiss her deeply. Who knew? He might even start talking more if she kept this up.

Chapter 14

Kirsten caught the bus down the road from the Jock's flat. He had given her some change, a couple of crisp £20 notes. In the rear of the bus, Kirsten tried to seem relaxed, but she was secretly scanning every passenger that got on. She could be being watched, being tested all this time, and the more faces she could clock from an organization, the better. Who knew when things like that would come back to hurt you? She wasn't the only one playing a game here; they were obviously playing one with her.

The bus made its way out of Fort William down towards Glasgow, and outside a small village, Kirsten found her stop. She had no name and she didn't recognize the road she was on. She was simply told to get off after so many stops once they had left Fort William.

There was a small wool shop at the stop and this was how Kirsten identified she had reached the correct one. Kirsten walked in a southerly direction along a small track that looked like it only had vehicles on the occasion when the fields around it demanded it. Maybe a tractor or a lorry taking the stock away to the processing plants.

A mile down the track, she made a right turn and saw a small cottage surrounded by a well-kept garden. It looked like a retirement house with neatly potted flowers all around it, a trim lawn, and no other buildings for miles. The whole setting was picturesque and quaint but in the driveway was a large black BMW. It should have been a sports convertible or an old Morris Minor, something nostalgic or sporty. That's what the house deserved, not this business vehicle that looked so out of place against the picturesque background. Then again, she was coming to see a woman who did not fit this house either. As Kirsten approached the front door and went to knock it, the door opened before her. She saw the man with black hair who had put a gun on her back the night before.

'Inside,' he said, looking beyond her, up and down the track. Kirsten stepped to the side and waited in a small hall with a decorative mirror on one side and a staircase that led up to a small landing.

'At the top,' said the man behind her, and Kirsten made her way slowly up the stairs. When she got there, she saw a door on her left, one on the right, and one in the middle of the landing. The one in the middle was half open and she could see a toilet and realised this was the bathroom. Turning around, she shouted back down to the black-haired man,

'Left or right?'

'Left,' he said dispassionately, then turned away from her.

Delightful, thought Kirsten. She turned and knocked the door she had been indicated to take.

'Come in.'

Kirsten opened the door and saw an all-white room with a number of computer terminals and also a large number of screens beside a desk. Before that desk was the blonde-haired woman from the previous night. She had a stylish set of black trousers on as well as a white blouse. Her heels were short and practical and she wore a pair of glasses. They were large and wide and caused her eyes to look larger than they were but her lazy eye still strayed.

'Jennifer, come in. Take a seat, please.'

Kirsten continued into the room and saw that there was a couch on the far side underneath the window. Overall, the room was compact but she could hear the whirr of hard drives and recognised most of the technology. It was up-to-date, modern, and Kirsten could see herself operating most of it, but she had to keep in character. She sat down on the couch looking at the woman, and gave her hands a little shake to indicate her nerves.

'Now, now, Jennifer, there's no need for that. You did well last night. Clever. Very clever, and that's why I want you to go and do another job for me. The Asian woman from last night needs to go north with her friends to be dropped off at a house further up. But first, you'll go over to Glasgow. I want you to keep the ladies in check. There'll be another colleague of mine coming along. He'll drive the minibus that'll take them up. Don't worry, they're all very good. Stay calm. They'll be dressed like they're tourists. You'll have the outfit of a rep on so it shouldn't get too frisky.'

'Is that it then? If I do this, I start to get a proper room.'

'Did Jock not look after you last night?' smiled the woman.

'He gave me his couch. It's not really a flat. That is what he promised.'

'You haven't proved yourself enough for that yet. You do this job and then one more and you'll be there, but we'll make sure you're not sleeping on the streets before that. Do you trust me, Jennifer?' asked the woman.

Kirsten sat back in the seat, wondering how to answer this.

Of course, she didn't trust her. But what should Jennifer think of her?

'I don't even know your name,' said Kirsten. 'It's hard to trust someone when you don't know their name.'

'It's part of the business, not knowing names. For instance, Jock, that's what they call him. That's how most of my people know him as but I know who he is. Very few others do. Does it bother you, the secrecy?'

'It will bother me a lot less when I get my own flat. Jock reckons you want me to drive for you; that's why I guess he wants somebody who understands, who knows how to handle themselves, not draw attention. He believes in this cause though, doesn't he, Jock?'

'As do I, Jennifer, as do I. Sometimes we believe in different ways of bringing it about but Jock's a good lad. He does an important job for us. Like you will.'

Kirsten stood up and looked out of the window.

'Yes, I do like the view,' the blonde-haired woman continued. 'The lady who used to live here did so well with the garden I felt that we really owed it to her once she died to keep it up.'

'Is that how you bought it?' asked Kirsten. 'She died and you got it after that?'

'Well, certainly those events but not necessarily that way around,' smiled the woman. 'She was another freeloader, another foreigner in this country. You can probably guess that I'm not keen on them.'

'I do believe in what the colonel said. He realised they were parasites,' said Kirsten. 'That's why I went along with Jock's offer because I had seen him at the meeting.'

'He did say you were a bit of a believer. I'm glad of that. Sometimes you have to believe to get through these things.

Sometimes we don't do nice things, but we trust in the result, trust in what's going to come. Do you understand that, Jennifer?'

'I guess I do.'

'Have you ever handled a weapon?'

Kirsten thought how she should answer this. The night before she had taken a gun and put it to the woman's head. Looking back, it would have been a ploy to not know what to do with it, keep the safety on, but instead she reacted. 'I have used one in my time,' she said.

'In anger?' asked the woman. 'I could tell you've certainly experienced a gun. You've seen one, but I don't think that you've used it in anger.'

'Well, not to kill someone but I do know how loud they are.'

'Good,' said the woman. 'Let's go get you a new one.' The blonde-haired woman stood up and then as she went to leave the room, Kirsten called to her.

'What do I call you? I'm not asking for your name. I'm just asking for something to call you because at the moment you're just a blonde-haired woman.'

'You can call me Liz,' said the woman. 'I always think Elizabeth is such a proper name, isn't it?'

'Liz it is,' said Kirsten and followed the woman down the stairs into a room at the rear of the house. Sitting on a table was a silver attaché case and Liz opened it. She waved Kirsten over to look inside. There was a small handgun with ammunition beside it.

'You hold it like this and load it like that, but I guess you're probably reasonably familiar with it. It's not an uncommon gun, is it?'

'I'm not sure I've handled one,' said Kirsten, which was a

clear lie because she was sure she had used one during her training. 'Can you just show me how it works?'

Liz smiled, picked up the gun and demonstrated how the magazine should be loaded. 'There you go,' said Liz, handing over the loaded weapon to Kirsten. 'See, that's how much I trust you.' Kirsten glanced across the room and saw the black-haired man, his hand on his weapon inside his jacket. *You don't trust me that much*, thought Kirsten.

'Thank you,' Kirsten said, 'but what can I do for you?'

'As I said you're going to run an escort for some women. Here's an address for you to go to in Glasgow. You'll need to make your way back, get the bus to Fort Willian and then get yourself across to the city. We'd drive you but we stay away from each other's vehicles as much as possible. When you get to the address, clothing will be provided for you. Tonight, in that suitable disguise, you'll make the move taking the women from Glasgow to a destination up north. Once you get to that destination, you'll hand back your disguise and you'll make your way back to Fort William. We'll have somebody meet you there. Maybe Jock, as you seem to be getting on so well. Can you do this for me, Jennifer? There shouldn't be any difficulties.'

Kirsten nodded, but kept her hands shaking. She felt that showing some sign of nervousness was always good in front of this woman.

'The driver may ask you to handle anything if things go awry. We're not expecting any trouble but if it does happen, don't be afraid to clean it up in the most calm and least attention-grabbing way, like you handled yourself the other night. I think she's quite grateful to you, actually, our Asian friend. I'd have to kill her if I had to put you down as well.' There was almost a sneer going across the woman's face and Kirsten got the feeling that she was not used to being disagreed with. Kirsten got the feeling that the woman could be thoroughly brutal.

'Well, that will be all,' said Liz. 'We'll see you shortly then. Good luck with your trip and remember, we'll get you a flat. Where would you like it? You ever been in Glasgow? Possibly Edinburgh? I think I've got openings in both.

'I feel that being a driver for you, I'd need to be close to you,' said Kirsten.

'I said you'd be a driver for me. I didn't say necessarily you'd be driving me but that's an understandable mistake. The sort of mistake I can forgive.'

The implication, thought Kirsten, *is there's lots of mistakes she wouldn't forgive.* With that, she pocketed her weapon, thanked Liz, and made her way out to the front door. Kirsten did not look back, but she went to the bus stop and had to stand for another hour before the return bus to Fort William.

She felt now could be a good time to go and dig up her keys, get her own car back but then again, if she was seen in a car, it would not be good. Despite this, she made her way out to the burial site of her belongings and picked up her mobile, taking out the SIM card from inside. It was a special SIM card and the number would ring directly in to Anna Hunt.

After recovering it, Kirsten made her way into town and bought herself a cheap mobile and stuck the SIM card inside. The device was small and discreet. At the tourist information office, she found the next bus across to Glasgow and then spent the afternoon parading around a number of shops. She bought herself a new t-shirt, leaving the old one in a bin and as she was trying some jeans in another shop, she saw someone

123

get into the cubicle beside her.

Kirsten stood in the mirror, jiggling around in jeans and she saw a face peering in. They were watching her, of that she was sure but only since she had been on the bus. Prior to that she had been clear in Fort William. Maybe they were worried about her doing a runner or maybe she had been spotted by Anna Hunt's people. It wasn't unusual for the service to be watching you, especially if they had not heard from you.

Whatever it was, Kirsten was playing the part of Jennifer and she was playing it to maximum. She treated herself to slap up meal. Wondering how she should kill the last few hours before her rendezvous in Glasgow, she made her way to the cinema and sat watching a rom-com for which she did not care. Instead, she sat, letting the idea of what was going on churn through her mind. If she could do this successfully, she might get in closer. They had said driver, they wanted a driver and it was for this hitman. Surely, all she had to do was get this next bit right.

Chapter 15

Kirsten left the movie house and made her way to an industrial estate on the south side of Glasgow. They were probably still tailing her, if they ever were before, but she didn't care, acting nonchalantly as she walked along, rounding first a large cake manufacturing site, and then another site that processed gas bottles. Beyond that was a simple warehouse, and Kirsten arrived at the gates to find them locked. On the far side of the gate was a push-button with what looked like a speaker above it. She pressed it gently. There was a crackling on the speaker.

'Yes?'

'I'm here for the trip. The trip up north.'

There was silence, and then Kirsten heard a little click and the sound of electric whirring. Turning around, she pushed at the gate and found it free to open. Once inside, she shut it behind her and made her way over towards the warehouse building that lay at the far side of a concrete area. As she approached the warehouse doors, they opened and Kirsten made her way inside in the darkness.

A flashlight was suddenly shown in her face. She reached up with her hands.

'Don't move. Hands by your side. Look at the light.'

'I can't look at the light,' said Kirsten. 'I'm like squinting my eyes.' Instead, she looked up just above it, and she could hear a satisfied 'Humph'.

'So, you're my partner for this evening, is it? You and me all the way up north. Well, don't get all too lippy, eh? Just keep it shut and we'll get on fine. Cargo's in the back. You want to inspect it for her first?'

That was an interesting turn of phrase, thought Kirsten. *He's obviously expecting somebody senior, someone linked in with Liz, even if he doesn't know her name.*

'Yes. Let's have a look at them then. I figure they're all secure.'

The lights suddenly flew on, and Kirsten saw a man standing close to her with a torch in hand. Now that the warehouse was lit up, she could see a minibus, and on board were a number of women. Making her way over to the bus, and not waiting for the man to follow, she opened the back doors and stared inside.

'Sit down, shut up, and don't say anything. It's a long trip, so let's have nothing untoward. You understand me?' Behind her, Kirsten heard the man grunt an approval and watched him walk around to the front of the minibus. She closed the rear doors behind her, made her way up to the passenger side, but saw the man pointing from behind the wheel.

'You get them doors, and then get the gear as well. We'll get underway. I'm not planning on stopping on the way up.'

'Is it a long trip?'

'She didn't tell you then? She tells less and less people, doesn't she? You're meant to be the one she trusts. Are you just testing me? Because I shouldn't tell you anything, should I?'

'No, you shouldn't,' said Kirsten, grinning at the man.

The man himself was probably just a little over twenty. He had dark brown hair and was wearing a heavy metal t-shirt and black jeans.

'Where's the outfits?' asked Kirsten.

'When we get going a bit. Mile or two from here. We'll look mighty suspicious driving out of a warehouse with them on.'

'All the same, stopping and changing right there in the open, it's not a good idea, is it?' said Kirsten.

'You think so? You think she wanted us to do it in here? I mean, I don't want to get it wrong.' The man was tense, and Kirsten could see that he'd recently shaved. She had no idea how much money the man would get for this trip, but he was clearly keen to please. Whether that was for the chance to work again, or whether just a chance to not disappoint someone who could quite happily put a gun to your head, Kirsten didn't know, but obviously, Kirsten was the one meant to take charge.

'In here. We'll get changed in here. Where's my outfit?'

'Under the passenger seat.'

'Fine,' said Kirsten, 'I'll get changed first, then I'll sit in the minibus with them while you get changed. Let's not hang about.'

'Fine with that.'

Kirsten reached under the passenger seat, pulling out a black bag.

'We are returning, aren't we?' she said.

'Yeah, round trip.'

'Grand, I'll leave my stuff in here. You can leave yours with it too. Don't bring anything that identifies you, you understand?'

The man nodded. Kirsten marched away through to an office at the side of the warehouse and quickly changed into a sharp skirt and blazer combo with an over jacket. She brushed her hair back, and found some lipstick and blusher inside the bag, and applied it in sensible quantities. There was also a set of high heels. Kirsten found that her foot size matched perfectly. *Had somebody been at her feet? Had Jock measured her up when she'd been asleep?* Clearly there had been serious planning with this; it wasn't just a haphazard uniform.

As soon as Kirsten re-entered the minibus, the man jumped out, ran round to the office and was back within five minutes in smart white shirt and black trousers, along with a jacket that bore the badge of a company that Kirsten had never heard of. She looked at her own jacket and realised she was sporting the same badge.

'Happy Tours of the Rising Sun? You cannot be for real,' said Kirsten.

'Well, they are all foreigners, aren't they? All from over there. What do you expect? Anyway, I don't think this lot will speak. Done these runs before. They're all too scared. I'm not sure what else they do with them, but whatever it is, it keeps them from talking.'

Kirsten turned around and looked at the man. 'I don't need to know what you've done before. I don't need to know what happens with them. All I need to know is that you're going to put that key in the ignition, you're going to start up this minibus, and we're then going to leave. You will then drive us there in as sensible fashion as possible, not breaking any speed limits. Are you clear with that?'

'Yes, ma'am.'

'Don't call me ma'am. You're a driver on a coach tour. Call me—' Kirsten stopped. She looked at the jacket that she was wearing, and there was a name badge in the bottom. Susan.

She said, 'Call me Susan. I'll call you—' She looked across at the man's jacket, 'Jeff. Okay, Jeff? At least we can talk civilly now. Keep it to a minimum.'

'You mind if I have the football on while we drive up?'

'Of course, I do,' said Kirsten. 'Why on earth would you be listening to the football driving this lot? You can put the radio on for them. Don't have it too loud. Keep an eye on your rear-view mirrors as well. Want to make sure we're not being followed.'

Kirsten jumped out and found it hard to march across in her high heels. She wasn't really prone to wearing anything fashionable, being much happier with some sensible hiking boots or trainers. But she knew how to perform as she strutted across, trying hard not to stride too far like she normally would in her trousers. Skirts like this weren't designed for that sort of thing.

Once at the warehouse door, she pressed a green button and the door rose up, allowing the man to drive the minibus out onto the concrete forecourt. After closing the door behind her, Kirsten continued to walk across the yard until she got to the gate, where she found a release button on the inside. Pressing it, she then opened the gate and allowed the man to drive the minibus out. Happy that everything was closed up behind her, Kirsten took her place at the front of the minibus, turned around, and looked at the Asian women.

'And we smile. You understand? We smile. You look out that window, you're smiling. You're on a trip. So, we smile.' One of the women at the rear scowled at her and Kirsten stared. 'You. I said you. You smile. Smile for me now.' The woman continued to glower. Kirsten moved her jacket to one side. The woman could see her weaponry inside. 'That's better,' said

129

Kirsten. 'That's a smile. Anybody else got problems smiling, we'll have a little chat. So, let's smile. Get this show rolling, Jeff. I'm already enjoying it too much.'

Jeff drove off, maintaining a steady pace until he made it out of Glasgow and started heading north, routing through Stirling up towards Perth before taking the A9 to the north. The man said nothing, staring ahead, driving, concentrating on what he was doing. Kirsten kept turning around and looking at the women who were mostly sitting calmly in their confinement. As they cleared Perth and started to head along on the A9, Kirsten spotted the traffic was building up behind them.

'A little too sedate, Jeff. I suggest you pick it up a bit. I'm sure we can get a sixty out of this minibus.'

'That's not why I'm going slow. I thought maybe I should pull over in a bit. Three cars back.'

Kirsten looked in the rear-view mirror. 'Seriously? How long?'

'He arrived just before Perth, stuck well to us. He keeps dropping back every time another car in front of him pulls away or parks up. Never more than two cars behind but doesn't get close. Always keeping that distance like someone's watching.'

'Are you sure, Jeff? I mean, really sure. We're not just being paranoid with this one?'

Jeff shook his head. 'I've done this too often. Sometimes you get followed.'

'Police?' said Kirsten. But she knew it wasn't. Wasn't their car and it wasn't their style.

'No,' said Jeff. 'Rival, definite rival. I reckon they're just casing us. Having a look to see what we're doing. She won't like that. You'll have to report it to her. But I reckon they'll tail us all the way up.'

'I take it we still have a significant distance to travel then?' asked Kirsten.

'Yes, a significant distance.'

'Well, let's keep it going for a bit. We're going to think about somewhere good to pull over, somewhere out of the way. I want one of those lay-bys that isn't just at the side of the road, goes in behind a lot of trees. Do you know of any up here, Jeff?'

Kirsten knew exactly where she wanted to pull over. She had travelled the A9 road many times since working out of Inverness, and the lay-by that she wanted to go to was currently about three miles away. However, Kirsten didn't want to give away familiarity with the area.

'It's just a little bit further up,' said Jeff. 'There's one you can pull in; there's trees at the side so most people from the road wouldn't be able to see.'

'Good, Jeff. Just before we get there, let's see if we can put a little distance between our tail. We've got to make sure they can see us when they go past. You understand what I'm saying?'

'Yes, create a gap, but then make sure he sees us in the lay-by so he has to double back, giving you time to get out and do whatever you want to do. I think you've done this before.'

'You don't have to think about anything, Jeff, except what I've just said to you.'

'Okay. There's no need to get shirty about it. I know my job. I'll do it. Don't worry. You do what you have to do.'

Kirsten sat in silence as the minibus rumbled on until she saw in the distance the lay-by at the side of the road. She felt Jeff put a little bit of pace into the minibus, and by the time he suddenly pulled to one side and entered the lay-by, he had significant distance between him and the car behind.

'Pull over.' Jeff did as commanded and Kirsten jumped out, fighting her high heels to race into the trees. As she looked out, she saw the car that had been following them go past the lay-by. She waited, assuming he would come back, and was not disappointed when two minutes later the car came and pulled into the lay-by from the far side of the road, a manoeuvre that was not legal.

Kirsten eyed the black BMW as it pulled up behind the minibus. She spotted the man in the front seat who reached down into the glove compartment, probably pulling out a gun. The man was alone, and Kirsten would have to play this smart. She waited until he got out, made his way around the back of the car, and then started to walk towards the minibus. It was late in the day and night had already fallen. There were no streetlights in this lay-by. Kirsten, as best as she could in her high heels, walked quietly up behind the man and placed her gun in the middle of his back.

'Yours in your left hand now or else I drop you here. It's a silencer. No one will know. Don't make me do it. Walk forward up to the side of the minibus. Keep your hands where I can see them.'

The man's left hand appeared with a gun. Kirsten took it from him and she then frog-marched him up to the front of the minibus. She opened the door and looked in at Jeff.

'Get on the move again. About four or five miles up, pull over again. I'll see you shortly.' With that, she shut the door. Jeff didn't hesitate and the minibus pulled away.

Kirsten pushed the man towards the hedge, insisting he force his way through to the other side. She watched him carefully, waiting for him to make a move. He must have thought he was heading to his grave, getting whacked, as the Americans would say. Any second now, he would try to reach around, try and do something that would overpower her.

Right on cue, as Kirsten was emerging from the hedge, the man spun around. He threw a fist towards Kirsten's gun and she parried it out of the way. Then the man carried through, stumbling forward. She gave him a kick in the backside. He then turned around to her, fists up. Kirsten hit him first with a left jab, once, twice, and then finished him off by slamming the gun butt across his cheek. He tumbled to the ground, motionless.

'Bad night, fellow. Not what you wanted to do. Now, what am I going to do with you?'

Chapter 16

The first thing that Kirsten Stewart did was to take off her high heels. She hated them. At one point, she thought she might overbalance when she turned to kick her foe in the backside, but she held her position and managed to knock the guy out. Still, she needed to do something with him. The trouble was, he was from a rival gang. If he had been government, she could have just phoned in, told him to lay off, maybe even let him come to, though without her ID, it would have been awkward. There was also the fact that Anna Hunt didn't want anyone knowing what Kirsten was up to. So really, it was probably the same whether he was government or not.

Kirsten heard traffic passing by on the A9 and tried to think hard about what to do. The guy needed to be out of the picture. If she was still involved, and the guy turned up alive, it would not go well. The man had seen her. More than that, he had seen Jeff, seen people working for the organization. Therefore, he needed to be silenced. Kirsten knew that Liz would expect that she would deal with him, in the most nefarious way. If Kirsten came back and the man was alive, it was likely that Kirsten would face a bullet.

There was also the question of his car. If she did kill the man, what would be done with it? Surely, there was some way to make this work. It struck Kirsten that the best thing was for this man to disappear, but also for people to think he was dead. She reached inside her jacket and picked up her new mobile with her work SIM card inside it. She dialled the number and waited for an answer.

'It's Anna. What's the trouble?'

'I'm working my way up. I'm involved in something to show I'm trustworthy and think I might be getting close to the person that might have set up this hit, but I need a favour.'

'What?' asked Anna.

'Kind of got a situation,' said Kirsten. 'I've got a guy knocked out at my feet. He should be dead. Clearly, I'm not going to kill him, so I need somebody to come and pick him up and stow him away for a while. I'll then burn his car out, and I want the police to say they thought there was somebody inside it. Can you make that happen?'

'What's your position?' Kirsten gave her location on the roadside. 'We're going to involve Richard. He's not that far away, but he could take a little time to get there. How long have you got?'

'Probably about five minutes, so he's not going to be here in time. What I'll do is I'll tie this guy up, hide him before I take his car. I'll burn it some distance away, so Richard won't have to worry about anyone giving him any hassle.'

'Good idea,' said Anna. 'I'll send Richard now. Where are you going to stow the guy?'

'Tell Richard there's a hedge on the other side of the lay-by. He has to go through it, and there's a copse of trees beyond it. The guy will be tied up there. I've knocked him out good, but I don't know how long he'll stay that way. I'll make sure he's secure. If anything goes wrong, text me. I need to know I've got my back covered. If this goes wrong, somebody will be after me.'

Kirsten made her way back to the man's car and found it still to be open. Checking the boot, she found some rope, some cloths, and a few concoctions that were designed to knock people out. Clearly, the man had come prepared. Looking along at a row of syringes, Kirsten made sure she pulled out one that would keep the man asleep for a long time. Just in case things went wrong, she took a rope as well to make sure he stayed put. She returned to the moaning man and injected him before tying him up. Searching his pockets, she took out a set of car keys and found a knife inside his trouser leg as well.

Returning to the car, she placed the knife in the well of the passenger seat along with the man's gun. Quickly she drove away, joining the A9 again and then turning off at the nearest village where she found a small garage still open. Kirsten pulled up alongside it but made sure her back window was rolled down. She looked over at the attendant in the building and started filling the car up but then indicated that something had got airlocked before lifting out the nozzle and placing it into the rear window. Again, she pulled the trigger, spreading the petrol about on the back seat. Once she thought there was a copious amount in there, she returned the nozzle back to refuelling the car before releasing the trigger at £20.

Replacing the nozzle, Kirsten left her jacket in the car, happy to not advertise her imaginary company, went inside the garage and paid cash. Once back in the car, Kirsten drove quickly with the window down to make sure the fumes from the petrol didn't overcome her. As she made her way up the road, she saw a minibus sitting at the side and pulled over beyond it into the lane of a farmyard. Taking her jacket, she put it back on and stepped out of the car, making her way back to the minibus and Jeff.

'You're not leaving that there, are you?' said Jeff.

'Nope. Do you smoke?' she asked.

Jeff nodded, 'I didn't think you'd want me to here.'

'I don't. Give me your lighter or your matches.' The man pulled a box of matches from his rear pocket and handed them to her. 'I'll only use one or two,' she said. 'You'll still have enough for your cigs when I get back.'

With that, she turned, marched back across in her high heels, and stood beside the rear window of the car. She struck a match, threw it inside, turned and walked away. By the time she got to the minibus, the car was heavily on fire. She threw the matches at Jeff.

'Let's go put some distance between us and this car.'

Kirsten grinned because there were no other cars passing by at the time on the A9. As they pulled away, she realised she had done it. She had made an effective cover story. Jeff was looking at her sullen, almost as if he dared not ask the question that was on his lips.

'He was inside,' said Kirsten.

'Hell, Susan. You're the business, aren't you? She'll be happy, the boss lady. He'll not follow us again. You really are some piece of action.'

'Just keep driving; get us to where we're going.' With that, Kirsten looked out of the window. In the rear, in the distance, the car was fully ablaze. It was up to Anna Hunt to spin her magic and Richard to pick up the man she had left behind. It was times like these you had to have trust.

As they continued up the A9, Kirsten fought hard not to

fall asleep. The journey was quiet now, the road in darkness. There was no one behind them, no car lights, and when she turned around to look at the Asian women, most of them were asleep.

'This definitely isn't your first run, though. Is it?' said Jeff.

'What makes you think that?'

'The way you handled it. Very smooth. I've been in with a lot of people doing this run. You know, I'm just a driver. I know I should keep my mouth shut, and I get from A to B. The people in that seat, they're the ones that deal with things. Some of them haven't lasted. Especially when we've had issues that weren't dealt with firmly. I think you'll be all right, Susan, though. That was very well handled.'

'Don't try and butter me up, Jeff. Just keep going.'

'Professional to the core. I like it,' said Jeff and turned the radio up. Kirsten wasn't sure what sort of music was playing, but Jeff liked it and he even began to drum occasionally on the steering wheel. Kirsten did wonder if this had been a setup. Had she been put on this minibus and given somebody to deal with? Jeff had said it was the enemy, a rival crew. Someone the boss didn't like. Kirsten had no other proof other than the man had got out with a gun and a knife in his trousers. He had also gone to the passenger side. *Was that the deal? He was sent to kill her so that she would kill him? Was he expendable? Was she expendable? Was it a case that if she didn't manage this, she wouldn't be worthy of the job she was being driven towards? Did Jeff know more than he actually said?*

There was no time to worry about this. All Kirsten could do was focus on what was in front of her. She recognised the drive down the large side of the mountain towards Inverness. There was some sparse traffic going across the bridge that

spanned the entrance to the Moray Firth, and when Jeff kept
the minibus chugging across it, she felt they might be going
much further north, maybe up towards Wick. But about two
miles later, Jeff took a turn at the roundabout and sent them
off towards Muir of Ord.

Before they could reach it, he made another detour into a
back road to a large farmhouse. On arrival at the farm, Jeff
stopped the minibus.

'You can go and tell them we're here; I'm not allowed to
get out. You'll have to escort them as I don't get to see who
operates this end of the operation, if you get my drift. As they
say, I just arrive in the warehouse down in Glasgow, and then
they turn up, tell me where to drop them, and I stay in the bus.'

Kirsten nodded and stepped out, making her way around
the bus and towards the farmhouse that was ahead of her. She
rapped in the door several times and finally it was opened by
a large woman who was dressed to impress.

'You here with a shipment, love?'

'How do you want them brought in?' asked Kirsten. 'They're
sat out there in the minibus.'

'You can just walk them in through here. It's fine. They
won't bat an eyelid. They're used to being moved about. We
got clients in tonight as well so just march them in. Oh, and
by the way, Susan, isn't it?' Kirsten nodded. 'You have to come
in with them. I've got instructions from the boss; we have to
look after you.'

'Why?' asked Kirsten.

'You should know by now that I don't get to ask why in the
same way that you don't. I have been told that you are to stay
here. I can't force you, I'm just asking you. I have a room
upstairs.'

Kirsten wondered what this was about. She was hoping she would end up back down in Glasgow that night, then get herself across to Fort William or maybe even end up in a hotel for the night. Anything to get her out of cover in some sort of way.

After standing for a minute thinking, she turned to the woman, 'Here it is then. Thank you. I'll just go and get these women.' Kirsten walked back, opened the rear door of the minibus, and escorted the women across. The large woman who had opened the door to her made sure they all came inside before offering the entrance to Kirsten as well.

'No, I've got to go and see Jeff and tell him to head back. He thinks I'm coming back with him.'

'Well, most of us aren't in the know. I guess he isn't either.' The woman closed the door. Kirsten walked back, stepping inside the minibus.

'Afraid you're on your own for the trip back; you okay with that? Do you need somebody to ride shotgun with you? I'll see if they've got anybody here if you want. Given the fact we've just burned somebody, maybe that could be wise.'

'That's all right. I'm just in a minibus. I'm driving down.'

'But they clocked our minibus. If they see it again and their man is dead, you could be a target.'

'She said bring the bus back, that's my job. If I don't do it that way, I'll be dead anyway. She doesn't like instructions being broken.'

Kirsten waved goodbye. As she made her way back over to the farmhouse, it dawned on her this probably was an entire setup. There's no way Jeff should be heading back with the minibus having been compromised. Certainly not on his own but he said he had been instructed to take it back. Anyone of reasonable mind would have turned round and said, 'No. Let's make a call. Let's make sure this is all right.'

Had the man been sent to kill Kirsten? It seemed so now. As if she was being tested. Was she worthy of looking after someone else? A shiver ran down Kirsten's spine as she realised she had been close to death again. As she approached the farmhouse, Kirsten shook her jacket and knocked on the door. The large woman opened it again and waved her inside.

'I'm afraid, love, as I said, we've got business tonight, so I'm not going to be able to talk to you. You're welcome to come down and sit with us. In fact, probably a good show if you did for a while. If you go upstairs, look for the room on the second floor at the far end, it'll have a number five on the door. That's yours. There are some clothes inside, should fit you. I suggest you wear one of the smarter numbers and come down. Just show face for a bit before going upstairs.'

Kirsten nodded and made her way up the farmhouse staircase. It was made of wood, and on either side, were very simple decorations such as horseshoes and pictures of straw bales and farmyard implements. When Kirsten reached the second floor, she turned right, made her way along following numbers that read from one to four until, at the very end, she found room number five. Opening the door, she found a pleasant room inside with a double bed, an ensuite, and a small desk. There were no pictures in the room, but there was a mirror on the ceiling causing her to think again about what the room was normally used for.

She made her way over to the wardrobe, opened the door, and found a red dress hanging inside. She looked around the rest of the room, but there was only a pair of jeans and a T-shirt. Deciding she needed to get tonight over more quickly, she changed out of her travel guide's uniform and slipped on the red dress that seemed to be cut a little bit too fine for her and certainly showing off more cleavage than Kirsten was comfortable with. In spite of this, she made her way downstairs five minutes later to be greeted by the large woman again.

'My name's Lucinda, and I look after this place. You're more than welcome, Jennifer. I just want to introduce you to some men I have in this next room. Don't be offended by what you see. At the end of the day, it's only the Asians, isn't it? They have to earn their keep here, but please, you don't. I just want you to show face, and then you can retire for the night. You must be tired.'

Kirsten agreed she was and followed Lucinda through to a room where five men were sitting in large chairs. Three of them smoked large cigars, and on the lap of each man was an Asian woman. To Kirsten's mind, it seemed that the women simply had not bothered to dress, but she tried to restrain her expression at what she saw as blatant slavery of a sexual nature.

'Gentlemen, I've been asked to introduce you to one of our new ladies but working on my side of the business, not that of the ladies on your laps. This is Jennifer. Say, "Hello," Jennifer.'

Kirsten held up her hand as if to wave and gave a brief hello. She watched Lucinda look around, gazing at each man in turn. Kirsten was aware she was being stared at, but unlike the attentions they had been giving to the Asians on their lap, the men were looking at her face. Kirsten understood what was going on. When one of the men turned around and said, 'Pleased to meet you,' Kirsten said, 'Likewise.' The greeting was followed by one in turn from each of the men, after which

Lucinda thanked Kirsten, saying she was free to go to her room. Kirsten acknowledged the men, turned around, walked out and up the stairs into her bedroom. Once there, she took out the gun she had, stood inside the shower, and waited to see if anyone would come into the room.

When after half an hour nobody had entered, Kirsten decided that she was okay. She had been paraded. These men, whoever they were, obviously knew operators and faces. Kirsten was new on the scene and clearly, nobody knew her yet. This may very well have just saved her life. She took off the dress, pulled on the t-shirt, and slipped inside the covers of the bed.She retained the gun under her pillow and didn't sleep very well that night.

There were plenty of sounds from below, even sounds from the next room, and at each loud one, Kirsten's eyes flew open to the door before her hand gripped the weapon beneath her pillow. Fortunately, each time she breathed a sigh of relief and closed her eyes again.

Chapter 17

As Kirsten awoke the next morning, there was a knock at her door. Without ceremony, a man stuck his head in, saw Kirsten under the covers and advised her that Liz was awaiting her downstairs at her earliest convenience. Kirsten thanked the man, waited until he closed the door, then threw off her covers, and made her way back to the shower in the ensuite. She washed quickly, before dressing in the t-shirt and leggings that have been left in the room. There was also a pair of trainers. Everything seemed to have been sorted for her, but Kirsten was aware that she was now wearing clothing supplied by these people. They could have put something in it to track her. She really would have to go dark now.

Making the phone call the previous night to advise Anna Hunt of the man she had tied up was a risk, but it was one that she had to take. If he had escaped, and was actually working for this group, then Kirsten's cover would have been blown. More than that, she probably would be dead. If he was not, and was working for someone else, then her lie about having finished him off would be found out, and she would be dead again.

Kirsten made her way downstairs. She could see the

remnants of what was quite a wild party but no one was moving about. Kirsten guessed that many of the guests were still in the bedrooms being entertained or were sleeping off the excesses of the night before.

When she reached the ground floor, the man who had stuck his head into her room pointed through the door at the rear that Kirsten had yet to enter. On opening it, she found a large kitchen in the middle of which sat a solid wooden table. The whole overall look was quaint, pots hanging down, and in the corner, a man in a white chef's outfit was cooking up eggs. At the far end of the table sat Liz, a neat jacket on, looking as ever, the businesswoman.

'Good morning, Jennifer. You've done well. I was particularly impressed that you didn't fluster on last night's run when one of our enemies decided to try and make a move. Have you ever worked much in the field of people trafficking?'

Kirsten shook her head. At least that wasn't a lie. She may have seen plenty of things as her time as a police officer, but she never worked in this field.

'You certainly handled yourself, and not afraid to get the dirty deed done, when you had to. I was wondering about that after you didn't shoot our Asian friend. I thought to myself, 'Does she have what it takes?''

'I've got what it takes to get to where I want,' said Kirsten. 'The flat, that's what I'm looking at. Steady job. Money. Doesn't matter to me about that bloke last night. He was coming to kill me anyway.'

'What makes you think that?' asked Liz

'Well, he had a gun out, and he was coming to my side. There was also a knife in his trouser leg. I see working for you can be quite risky.'

'Is that a problem?' asked Liz.

'No. Knowing the risk ahead of time would help though.'

The chef turned around and placed some scrambled eggs on a plate with some neatly arranged toast behind it. This plate was then offered in front of Liz. He turned around and asked Kirsten if she would be eating. Kirsten nodded. The man produced more scrambled egg on toast, setting a place just across from Liz at the large wooden table. When he had also placed a jug of filter coffee and several cups on the table, Liz dismissed him curtly.

'One of the good things about running places like this, you don't have to make your own breakfast.'

'I think you're in it for more than just a free breakfast,' said Kirsten and saw Liz's face sharpen.

'What do you mean by that?'

'We're here for a political end, aren't we? We're here to advance things. Here to change things. Not to simply make money. Don't get me wrong, I understand this, what we're doing, we have to finance a revolution. Finance changing things. I mean, who cares that these Asians have to go through a little pain to do that?'

Liz smiled. 'You're sharp, aren't you? Of course, we have the political end. We make things happen. You're going to help make something happen.'

'What's that?'

'You'll see,' said Liz. 'In fact, you're going to be a key player now that I know I can trust you. I need you to go and pick someone up for me down in London. I know you've been traveling back and forward these last couple of days, on the move, but you can take your time going down today. He's flying in tomorrow morning. Five o'clock in the morning.'

'Where from?' asked Kirsten.

'You don't need to know that. In fact, I don't need to know that. All he said was to be at Gatwick Car Park and he'll find you, five a.m. and not to be late.'

'Do I get to ask who he is or what he looks like just in case he doesn't find me?'

'He'll find you. Don't worry. He may also be a little bit touchy.'

'Touchy?'

'As in you might have a gun put in your face until you can identify who you are.'

'How do I do that?' said Kirsten. 'I mean, I wouldn't want anything to go wrong, for him to get trigger happy.'

'You tell him the Ratchet sent you.'

'The Ratchet? Is that you?'

'I think that's enough, don't you?' said Liz. 'The Ratchet sent you.'

'Then what am I meant to do with him?' asked Kirsten.

'You take him where he asks. Wherever he asks, for as long as he asks. Understood?'

Kirsten nodded. 'I pick him up, take him where he wants to go. Don't ask any questions. Once I've dropped him off?'

'Make your way back to Fort William. Go see Jock. You'll get your reward there. I hope you haven't got a problem living on the west coast. It'll be a nice flat, everything a girl could want. I'll get you a car too because you're going to run more errands beyond this. Here.' Liz threw an envelope in front of Kirsten. 'Something to look at while you enjoy your scrambled egg.'

Kirsten looked inside the envelope as Liz stood up. She could see a large number of notes but didn't count them.

'Call that an advance payment, something to keep you going.

147

Have you got a mobile number? Just in case we need to get hold of you,' asked Liz.

'Yes. I've got one, bought it recently with the cash I got earlier. Been a while since I've had one. I'll just need to check the number. I don't know it yet.'

'Not a problem.'

Liz watched as Kirsten pulled her mobile out and looked through the details until she got the number. The phone was dual sim, and the one that had been supplied by her employers didn't show up even though it was working. The other sim, that had come with the phone, had yet to be used but Kirsten passed the number over. In her head, she understood that this was not a mere courtesy or some sort of escape plan. She thought that maybe they would be able to ping it, follow it somehow.

'You'd better finish your eggs and get moving. You have two countries to get through today. There's a car outside and the man coming knows what it is. He knows the number plate and registration and as I said, he'll find you. Park in one of the car parks at five o'clock. Take him where he wants to go. Go back to Fort William, see Jock. You good with all that?'

Kirsten nodded. 'Yes. Thanks.'

'Thanks for what?' asked Liz.

'Trusting me, giving me a chance—hasn't happened in a while.'

'When I look at you, I think you can handle yourself,' said Liz. 'You handle yourself with your mind, with your emotions. You can control the way your face looks. The other night you were panicking. You haven't killed someone before, have you?'

Kirsten shook her head. 'Yet the other night, when you had to kill someone, you did it. You did it without hesitation. I

148

don't see you as a seasoned player in this game, but you're learning fast, Jennifer, and that I like. Just stay loyal. If you stay loyal, people will look after you. Don't mess about and don't betray us. That earns a swift party, and usually one you don't walk away from.'

Kirsten nodded and began to eat her eggs as Liz left the room. When she finished breakfast, Kirsten made her way out the front door, aware that she was being watched. A man, who the previous night had been a guest, had made his way downstairs. As Kirsten walked past, he tried to reach out and grab her, still drunk from the night before. She caught his hand and moved it gently to one side and pushed him into a seat. As she did so, the lady of the house appeared.

'Jennifer, sorry about that. Come on, Mr. Umbridge. I think you've enjoyed things a little too much.' The man stood up and kissed the woman on the cheek. 'I believe your playmate was upstairs, not down here. Jennifer here isn't for playing with. She might take exception to you playing with her, so let's get you to a place where you are safe to play.'

Kirsten felt reviled by the man. In fact, she felt reviled by the place. Women brought here to entertain. She would make a note of it all, make sure it was relayed back to people, but it would have to be done in a timely fashion as soon as they understood Kirsten's cover. Operations could be wound up, places would be moved, and the women who were being abused and used would be moved on. The undercurrent in the country of people trafficking was bigger than people knew.

Kirsten had thought once of joining the departments that looked after that side of criminal business. It would be exciting, fresh, to release people tied up in bondage. But Macleod had come along, and she had joined the murder team. Then this opportunity came. Was she not making a difference already? She hoped so.

The car outside was a Vauxhall. Kirsten read the number plate and understood it to be six years old. That was reasonable. It wasn't flashy, nothing about it said, look at me, yet it was probably extremely reliable.

The keys were sitting in the ignition, and when she turned it, she found there was a full tank of petrol. Kirsten pressed a button and when the sat nav came on and she simply typed in 'Gatwick Airport'. It took a moment for the system to calculate her best route, and then she drove off. She knew the route once she got to somewhere sensible, such as Inverness, but now on the outskirts, she wasn't quite sure where she was. Looking at the map, she clocked where the house was located, making a note of it to be passed on.

Kirsten was aware that eyes were watching as she drove out of the driveway of the house and onto the backcountry roads, and then soon out to the A9 heading south. She passed Aviemore where she previously had tailed Peter Harborough. The day was cloudy as she continued south. Kirsten had to be at Gatwick at five a.m. She wondered what was the best way to do this. She didn't want to arrive at Gatwick exhausted.

She drove, continuing her journey down, before she arrived just outside London just before seven o'clock. She found a small commercial hotel and picked up a room, getting her head down until three o'clock in the morning. Kirsten was sure she was being watched when she looked out of her hotel room at three a.m. and saw a car in the car park, one she recognised from being on the road along the A9.

When she got into the car to drive to Gatwick Airport, this strange blue sedan followed her until she parked up in one of the car parks, at which point it drove off. Clearly, the man arriving must have been a special package, and they wanted nothing to go wrong. Kirsten sat in the driver's seat looking at her watch. Five minutes to five. As the minutes ticked by towards the hour, Kirsten put the radio on, and tried to appear as casual as possible, but she was looking at every mirror, assessing who was coming close.

A man in a dapper grey suit appeared. He had a sharp chin and nose, his features cutting. He was clearly in good shape, and there was something in his eyes that seemed to stare. Kirsten ignored how he looked and stepped out of the car, opening the boot. The man walked up and asked did Kirsten know where to get a taxi.

'The front of the terminal, but Ms. Ratchet would probably prefer you take a car.'

He nodded, placed a briefcase into the boot of the car followed by some luggage that had been hanging in a bag off his shoulder. After that, he left Kirsten to close the boot and made his way into the passenger seat. When Kirsten joined him, he turned and extended a hand.

'Lars Franklin. Pleased to meet you.

'And you. I'm Jenn.'

'Just Jenn?' said the man.

'Yes, just Jenn, Lars. Obviously, that's the name I'll use for you, you use Jenn for me.'

The man nodded and then sat back in his seat, leaving Kirsten to drive off. Kirsten left the access road from Gatwick and approached the motorway . She asked Lars which direction to take. He advised they should head north, to Scotland, and he would tell her further once they were reaching the border. Kirsten nodded. They soon began to drive out of London on the motorway, heading North. As they passed Birmingham, having cut across country on Lars's instruction, Kirsten was aware that there was a car, maybe four or five back, that seemed to be continuing with them. Being the motorway, she was unsure whether it was not just a fellow driver on a long journey north, but they seemed to be persistent.

'Lars, I think we have a tail. I'm going to come off here, and I'm going to lose him because I think it's police.'

'Why do you think it's police?' Lars asked.

'It's just a thought. I don't know anybody else trying to stop you doing what you're doing because I don't know what you're doing. However, most of what I've been involved in, in the last couple of days, certainly wouldn't have been something that the police would like. I wasn't followed on the way down, so maybe they were watching you come off the flight.'

'It's a wise thought,' said Lars. 'Okay, you have my permission to lose them.'

My permission? thought Kirsten. *That wasn't the deal here, was it? This man, he wasn't part of the organization; he didn't phone up and check whether it was okay. He was looking after himself, for his own safety and security.*

Kirsten pulled off at the next junction, and sure enough, the car followed. She then drove off into the country roads, suddenly increasing speed, and still the car followed. Kirsten was an assured driver, and once she made sure that the car couldn't see her, she cut off into the driveway of a house. Luckily there were no other cars in the drive, even at nine o'clock in the morning, so Kirsten managed to get her car around the rear of the house via its extended drive.

Kirsten exited the vehicle, made her way to the corner, and

glanced around to see the pursuing car drive past the house. She ran back into her own car, reversed it and followed the road in the opposite direction back towards the motorway. Kirsten found a car park not far from a hire car service. Together with Lars, they parked up a little way from the hire company. Lars insisted that he take out the hire, produced documents and cash, and soon they were driving away again, this time in a small rented hatchback.

'Very neat,' said Lars. 'They won't be able to chase me through the rental, don't worry about that. I've done this before many times.'

There's a slight accent in the voice. Why Lars? Why would you say that? If you are in Scotland, why not Steve, Ian or Eric? Clearly the man was not that bothered and there was a certain assuredness about him. They continued to drive north and arrived into Inverness at about six in the evening, at which point Kirsten asked where to next.

'I believe you know. I was told to ask you, take you to where you wanted to be, drop you off, and then head elsewhere,' said Kirsten.

'No. You get to take me to where you were last night.'

Kirsten smiled. Once again, she was being played, kept in the dark about future plans. Had she arranged for people to go and meet her in Fort William, she would have been watched. Even meeting Jock, she would have been watched. Her cover would have been blown and all chance of tailing these people would inevitably fall apart.

When they arrived at the farmhouse, Kirsten took Lars's cases in for him. Arriving at the front door, Lars was greeted by Liz and taken away to a separate room, while Kirsten was advised that Lars's room would be the one that was next to hers. She made her way up the stairs and placed Lars's bags within his room. Looking at the briefcase, Kirsten thought about opening it, but it was too much of a risk.

Kirsten returned downstairs but was advised by the woman of the house to return to her room where in the wardrobe, she would find a dress for dinner. She was asked to attend at nine o'clock. Kirsten smiled and nodded, but she desperately wanted to find out what Liz was saying to the man. However, Kirsten was tired, so she laid back in her bed in her room before making her way over to the wardrobe and beginning to dress for that night. She should take a shower, after all. She had to make it look like she was enjoying this life, not simply trying to find things out. She also needed to be ready to make a move, even though she was still in the dark about what Lars was here to do.

Chapter 18

Kirsten put on the high-heeled shoes that were in the wardrobe as well as a black dress. It was strapless and clearly there to accentuate her figure, which made Kirsten very wary. Why would she be in a dress like this? Who was she going to see? After all, she was in an illegal brothel, a place where women were observed and used. If she was to become one of these women, she would need to get herself out, and quick.

At nine o'clock exactly, she made her way down the stairs where she found a house full of clients and the Asian women working again. She was guided to a room at the back where she found Liz sitting in a study. The door was closed behind her. Liz did not look up from her desk, instead looking at papers in front of her. Kirsten could not read them, but she made her way over to sit on a small wooden chair.

'Jen, well done today. I'm impressed. Lars told me about the police tail and how easily you shook it off. I got one of the boys to return the hire car. Lars is heading off tonight, but I won't need you to run him. He'll be going off on his own, but you've done your job and you've done it well. In the morning you can head back over towards Fort William and meet Jock.

You'll have your flat there.'

Kirsten watched the woman. There was something different about her tonight. Previously she had been all business, but now there was a gleam in her eye as if she was waiting for something.

'Stand up, Jen. Come with me.'

Kirsten was surprised when the woman put her hand out to Kirsten's and led her like they were a pair. She walked through the house smiling at clients who were sitting on chairs with Asian women fawning over them. Liz stood at one end of one of the rooms, Kirsten beside her and Kirsten felt a hand run up and down the middle of her back. Was this a side to Liz that Kirsten didn't know? Was the woman in some way interested in her, even if only for some sort of temporary use?

Kirsten felt a chill in her spine, but she let Liz continue to put her hands on her shoulders before she let her back into the study again. Once inside and the door closed, she called Kirsten over to the window and had her look out onto the neatly lit lawn. With hands on Kirsten's shoulders, Liz began to talk into her ear.

'I've worked hard for this,' she said, 'to get to a place where I can get what I want. You said it was all about the cause. There's nothing wrong with being able to have something of your own while you fight that cause. I like to own things,' said Liz.

Kirsten felt the hand move down her arm and towards her hips.

'I like to know that things are mine. Are you mine, Jen? Everything you've done, you've done for me and you've done well. You seem to understand and know what I want.' A second hand slid down onto the other hip. 'I like someone who pleases me, especially someone with curves like this.'

Liz was taller than Kirsten, shoulders about the height of Kirsten's head. The woman had to bend down to keep her hands on Kirsten's hips. The hands then moved, continued upward to a place where Kirsten was not comfortable.

'I like to own people,' said Liz. 'They're in my pocket and I reward them. I reward them very well. They can have cars, houses, clothes, whatever they want. I even sort out other problems for them. Have you got problems to be sorted, Jen? Oh, Jen, you really have been quite a find. I spoke to Lars tonight. What'd you think of him? Was he professional?'

'Yes' said Kirsten, her hand moving up to take hold of Liz's and try and move it down from where it was trying to reach inside to Kirsten's breast. 'Very professional. Spoke nothing about the job and he's not called Lars, is he? He did nothing spectacular. When we were being pursued, he was as calm as anything, assessed the plan, and then made his decision.'

'Would he be good for us? Do you think he would lie and betray us in if caught?'

'I don't know what he's doing,' said Kirsten.

'Something illegal. Very illegal,' said Liz. 'Do you think he would be a grass if they caught him?'

'No,' said Kirsten. 'He seems professional to the core.'

'So, you think we can trust him?'

'I think he's as good as the money you're paying him. I think if you didn't keep your side of the bargain up, he would react.'

'He's cost a lot of money to bring in, but they say he's good, very good which is a pity. Sometimes politics and personal pleasure don't mix, Jen. Sometimes you have to sacrifice something personal.' Kirsten felt hands gripping her tighter before suddenly, Liz's right hand moved away. 'Sometimes even something lovely has to be disposed of.'

157

Kirsten was on edge when she felt Liz step away slightly. She decided there was no risk worth taking here and she stepped forward just out of Liz's reach. Liz stumbled behind her. Kirsten spun around and saw a knife in Liz's hand. Liz brought her arm up to strike Kirsten in the face, but Kirsten was too quick for her. She grabbed Liz's wrist and kicked her hard into the midriff. The woman fell forward and Kirsten instinctively moved closer. Her mixed martial arts training was coming into use now. She followed through with punch after punch to the face, causing Liz to tumble backwards at the study desk and then fall off to the side.

Liz cried out. Kirsten could hear footsteps coming already. She kicked off her heels, reached down and grabbed the knife that had fallen from Liz's hand, and made her way to the window. Without hesitation, Kirsten threw it open and jumped out into the night. She skirted away from the neatly lit lawn and found herself running over hard stones. Her feet screamed as she tried to scan around to see what was ahead.

Kirsten could run out the front gate, but surely, they would have the cars on the go soon. She did not want to give them any advantage. Looking to her left-hand side, she saw the edge of the farmhouse where a fence led out into a field. Although dark, the clouds had opened up and there was enough moonlight to see by. Kirsten hitched up her dress, which went just past her knee. She couldn't run fully with it like that. Hoisting it up to her hips, Kirsten started to run hard across the field. Behind her, she heard a commotion as she jumped across the fence.

Something brushed the trees beside her. Kirsten believed it was a gunshot used with a silencer. She kept low as she tried to run away. Obviously, Lars was the one here to do a job.

Kirsten had seen him; therefore, Kirsten had to be put down. Liz was regretful about this because she had seen something in Kirsten she liked. Not necessarily something that Kirsten wanted her to like, but thankfully, it had given Kirsten that moment. She felt the thick mud on the ploughed field.

Kirsten continued to run, unsure of where the road was. She struck off across the field to the far corner. Behind her, she could hear people coming but she wanted to get somewhere where there were trees, somewhere where she could have some sort of an advantage to fight back. She was carrying no weapon in the dress she had worn, and it did not allow for a holster anyway. On reaching the far side of the field, Kirsten made her way behind a tree and looked back to see who was arriving. There were three men pursuing her, all holding guns but one was out ahead of the rest.

She remained behind the tree as the man made his way towards it. He arrived and stopped slowly, trying to look around the tree. Kirsten grabbed him. Her arm around his neck slowly drained the life out of him. She knew how to choke somebody hard, how to render them unconscious and how to keep on doing it until they died, but she didn't have time for that.

Once the man's struggles were starting to fade, she let her arm go and simply punched him hard across the face several times. He was out cold, but he made a noise during the fall, and she heard gunfire, the bullets whispering through the trees, shot by silencers again.

Kirsten ran, but this time she kept to the wooded path that lay behind the trees as it turned this way and that. Eventually, she saw a chance to climb a tree. Ripping off the bottom of her dress, she threw it down onto the path. This allowed her the freedom to move her legs up and climb unrestricted. The two men who'd been following her had obviously found their colleague because when they saw her dress lying in the path, they approached it cautiously. They hunted here and there around the tree. Only when they passed her by a few steps did Kirsten react. Jumping out of the tree she landed blows in both their backs before they could react. She punched one, then the other, then back to the first one again. Like a whirling dervish, she hit and kicked until both were lying on the ground.

Kirsten then struck blows to their heads that incapacitated them. She grabbed their guns, threw them out into the trees, and ran off as hard as she could. She reached the end of the path and a car park. There was a road beyond, and she ran onto it, sticking to one side, but continuing in that direction as far away as she could from the car park. Others would follow, they would find, and they would then pursue further. Kirsten's hope was she could flag someone down before that.

Although dark, it was not that late for light traffic. Kirsten was hopeful that even here in a back country lane, there might be a car shortly. But none arrived, and the sweat poured off her as she continued to jog hard. Her bare feet were sore, cut and bruised from running on such hard ground.

Up ahead, she saw the lights go past of cars moving quickly. It was a main road. Kirsten felt like crying, bursting into tears at the lights. Unless she ran out into the road, she wondered how she could flag someone down. Surely the state she was in, someone might stop. Her dress, which she had ripped, was now up past her hip. Frankly, she looked like someone who had been mugged, but she didn't care. As long as someone stopped, she could escape.

As she arrived at the main road, stumbling along, there were lights behind her. She ran out quickly and then back off the road, causing the vehicle to stop. A door was flung open.

'Are you okay, love?' said a woman's voice.

'He's after me,' said Kirsten. 'After me. Take me away.' With that, she fell towards the woman. She helped Kirsten up and into the camper van that the woman had emerged from. Once inside, Kirsten saw the man behind the wheel stare at her.

'Bloody hell, love, what have you been up to?'

'He's after me.'

'Right,' said the man, 'I'll sort him.'

'No,' said Kirsten. In her own mind, she knew that would be the worst of all worlds. These two people could end up dead. As Kirsten insisted the man go, something hit the side of the camper van, and it was shunted off the road, running into a tree.

Kirsten's head had thrown forward and hit the dashboard, stunning her. As she tried to come to, a face could be seen as the door opened. It had black hair, tightly cropped and Kirsten recognised the man from the farmhouse.

Chapter 19

Kirsten's head was ringing like she had been hit with a cold punch inside her martial arts ring but she had not taken a pounding within those fighting arenas without being able to develop the nuances of a quick recovery. The man from the farmhouse reached in and saw Kirsten, and grabbing her by the hair, he pulled her out.

Kirsten stumbled out as if she didn't know what was going on but inside she was just biding her time. Once her feet had hit solid ground, she threw an elbow into the midriff of the man causing him to double over. He still had a gun in his hand, as no doubt his other colleagues around the campervan did. Kirsten put her hands behind his head pulled it down before driving her knee up into his face. There was a sickening thud as her knee smashed his nose into oblivion.

The driver of the camper van looked on in shock but Kirsten pushed him forward telling him to get out of the way. She moved closer to the campervan anticipating someone coming around it and sure enough, another of the men from the farmhouse stepped around. Kirsten caught him with a knee into his stomach, then hit him on the back of the head. He dropped down and she stamped into his back. She heard a crack but didn't stop to wonder what it was. Instead, she reached down and grabbed his gun, and put her back up against the campervan again.

They would be coming for her, but she looked quickly underneath the campervan, seeing a number of legs on the other side. The legs were starting to run and soon she would be overwhelmed with three or four people coming at her.

She put her head back underneath the campervan, targeted the legs, and fired several times. There were cries, shouts of pain, and people falling over. She could hear the woman from the campervan shriek and her husband crying back to her. A couple, maybe in their fifties, but Kirsten knew as much as she wanted to help them, her first priority would be to get away.

She had information on a possible attempt on the life of someone high up in public life. Kirsten had a duty to report that as well as the location of the people traffickers but there was something else inside of Kirsten. She had been taught decency by her previous employer. Macleod had always stood up for the innocent and as grumpy a man as he was, he was upright in his standing. A dinosaur when it came to political correctness but a champion when it came to defending the weak.

Kirsten edged around the campervan. Two men were lying on the ground and one spun over to raise his gun towards her. She ducked back and heard a shot go off before returning and firing at the man, a double shot to his temple. From the shape of his head afterward, Kirsten knew he was dead. There was movement from behind the campervan and around the corner came one of the men holding the woman from the campervan at gunpoint. The woman's blonde hair was being held behind her, gun in her ear. Kirsten could see her terrified face with tears streaming down it.

She held her own gun right up in front of her. *How would she play this? What should she do?* The man with the hostage smiled at her.

'Not so easy when we've got somebody innocent.' he said. 'I said all along you were too good to be true. I said all along you were—'

The man's body hit the ground making the woman jump. Kirsten was fighting back the reaction to shake, to cry out. She had just killed two men, her first time, the first time she had reacted with such violence but too much was at stake.

She grabbed the woman who was standing, crying. As Kirsten moved away, she struggled to pull the woman after her, in her ripped dress and bare feet. Kirsten knew she had to get away from the scene, but also to take these people out of the way. The man was standing some distance from the campervan looking back in horror, and when he saw his wife his tears started to roll as well. Kirsten looked around her. There were four men on the ground, two cars behind her. *Was that it? Would there be more coming?* She started to cross the road, saw a car coming from the other direction and the couple began waving frantically.

Kirsten's mobile was back in the farmhouse but she had taken precaution before leaving, placing the SIM card inside her underwear in a small flap where the elastic ran around her waist. As she had no phone, there was no way of contacting headquarters or the police. As the car came closer to them, Kirsten hoped it was not any of the crowd from the farmhouse. It was coming from the opposite direction but who knew where they had people; maybe they had called others in. When the car stopped, Kirsten saw it was a family, a man and his wife, baby in the back, and another kid.

The woman sitting in the passenger seat rolled down the window, her hair was tied back. She looked out with inquisitive eyes at the sobbing man and woman and then looked strangely at Kirsten in her half ripped dress.

'What the hell's going on?' asked the woman. The lady from the camper van went to reply, but Kirsten instead started barking orders at the driver.

'Open your boot, get the boot open and you two get inside.'

The man and the woman while still crying turned to look at Kirsten as if she was mad.

'I mean it. Get in the boot. Once you're inside, you, behind the wheel, turn around, keep going until you find a police station. When you're there, stop and take these two inside and they'll tell them what's happened. But get out of here now!'

'Why should I? I'll phone the police, love. I'll stay here and phone the police.'

Kirsten looked at the man behind the wheel imploringly with her eyes. 'Do as I say. There are two dead men over there wearing bullets.'

'And who shot them?' asked the woman.

'I did. Get out of here!'

'There's no way,' said the man, 'I'm calling the police.'

Kirsten raised the weapon, holding it inside the window. 'Those two in the boot, turnaround, drive, get the police, or I will shoot you and drive you there myself.'

The mother began to shake, pushed herself back in the seat, and turned to look at her husband. 'Just do it, just do what she says; she's already nuts—just do it.'

'You two get in the boot.' Kirsten watched the campervan couple get inside the boot, close it, and then the car sped away.

As it disappeared back from where it came, she heard other cars coming from the opposite direction. Kirsten turned and ran into the nearby hedge. Fighting through the scratches, she emerged on the other side and began running across another ploughed field. As she continued, it began to rain, with a wind beginning to pick up. Although she was running as hard as she could, legs pounding, she could still feel the cold of the driving rain as it began to pour from the heavens above.

She needed to orientate herself. She was near Inverness, there were going to be safe houses, but she needed to find where she was. Kirsten continued along the field keeping a small country road on her right-hand side. As she ran, she saw a bus stop, but rather than looking for a ride, she ran over to the transparent facility and began scanning what routes were pasted.

I'm near Muir of Ord, she thought. *If I keep going this way, it might just lead me towards the village*. With renewed vigour, Kirsten fought on, keeping off the road and continuing across the fields. She had not seen a sign, so kept going until she descended down a hill and recognised the road ahead of her. *There, take a right and the house will be just up and along*, she thought.

There was a safe house in Muir of Ord she had used before. It was basic, but it was shelter and it had a phone. Kirsten's head was still ringing, and she promised to get herself looked at whenever the cavalry arrived, but until then, she persisted and emerged out on the side of the main road into Muir of Ord.

Three more houses up, she thought, but then she saw a man wandering around the corner.

Kirsten had planned to keep out of the way, not to be seen

by anyone, as it's hard to answer questions when you're only wearing a ripped dress. She was soddened and looked like the wildest of Friday night partygoers. In fact, she would not wear something like this to a club. As she walked along, the man got closer, and she saw him swaying across the pavement from left to right. As she approached, he stopped.

'My word, that's a belt not a skirt,' he said. 'Game on, love, game on.'

Kirsten laughed as she walked past, and when she was quite sure he was heading the other way and not looking back, she made a right turn through a small gate and up to the house that belonged to the service. She disappeared around the back and found the key hidden under a rock in the flowerbed. Opening the rear door, she made it inside, locked it, and then went upstairs.

Kirsten picked up the phone that was located upstairs and dialled the number for headquarters. Inside thirty seconds, she was speaking to Anna Hunt. Kirsten distilled the situation to her and heard her drawing breath.

'Great. You've lost him. He could be anywhere. Do you hear me? You had him in your sights. You were with him, and you've lost him. Will you be able to find him again?'

'I don't know at the moment, okay? I don't know. I can't think straight. I can't think straight.'

'Well, you better sharpen up. I'll send Richard round.'

'Send the doctor. I cracked my head. It needs to be looked at.'

'No, I won't. Nobody knows what you've been doing, where you've been. We're keeping this quiet. I'll send Richard with a medical kit.'

The phone went dead. Kirsten tried to stand up but it wasn't the bang in the head that was bothering her. Instead, she started to see the two men, the pair she had shot. Kirsten had been extremely proficient, dealt with them in the way she had been trained, but these were the first people she had ever killed. They deserved it, scumbags, ready to kill her. They were ready to kill the innocent people in the campervan who had just been in the wrong place at the wrong time. Good people who stopped to help her.

Kirsten stumbled to the shower but she did not take off the dress. It was only her training that made her reach inside her underwear and lift out a little SIM card for the phone and place it to one side. She switched on the tap, pulled up the button and she heard the water falling into the bath from the shower nozzle. Kirsten pulled back the curtain, stepped inside, and let the water hit her. Afraid she would fall over, she simply sat down, head in hands, and began to cry.

She heard the knock at the door but she could not get up. She hoped it was not anything untoward, hoped it was just Richard coming. Two minutes later, the door of the bathroom opened.

'Are you okay?' he asked.

'You can come in,' said Kirsten. 'I'm decent.'

Richard walked in. As she turned to look at him, she saw his face and he was a little bit puzzled, to say the least.

'That's a different sort of shower outfit.'

'I couldn't take anything off. I couldn't do anything. I couldn't…'

The man stepped forward and turned off the shower.

'You're in shock and you need to calm down. We need to get you somewhere to rest. Out you come.'

He helped her get out of the bath and to stand up fully.

Stripping her completely, he began to rub her down with a towel from the room. There was nothing indecent about what he did, just simple practical help, almost as if he had been a nurse. When he had finished, Richard wrapped the towel around her and told her to go and sit on the bed in the adjoining room.

As she sat there, the faces came out at her again and Kirsten felt the tears streaming down her face. She didn't hear Richard come in, but she noticed a cup of tea placed in front of her and took it gladly from him, sipping on it gently.

"You need to stay put," said Richard. "I'll take care of you, but we need to stay here for an hour to get you sorted."

'Anna's angry, said we lost him, said I lost him.'

"Anna's always angry," said Richard. "You got to look after yourself. When we get a minute, you can give me some descriptions and details. At that point, we'll start to worry about what's next. For now, don't worry at all.'

'I can't believe I did it. It was just like he was standing there holding a gun to her head and I just blew him away while he was speaking.'

'You did right, and you did clever," said Richard. "You're alive and your hostage is alive. That's your job. Don't beat yourself up over things that you couldn't do anything else about it. There's enough that goes wrong in this job. Enough regret."

The words seemed to fall on deaf ears because no matter how much she thought about it for the next hour, all Kirsten could see were the faces of dead men looking back at her.

Chapter 20

T
rue to his word, Richard had given her a couple of hours before he started questioning her about the individual she had picked up. Kirsten ran through the type of car she had driven up in, though they doubted that the man was still driving the same one. She spoke of a briefcase and of how he looked. Lars had been thin, but strong, composed, and professional. Richard sent the description back to Anna, who was checking through records from Gatwick, scanning photographs of people who had come through, but Kirsten was doing nothing.

She was sitting on the bed thinking about what had happened, thinking about her escape, feeling the bruises on her feet and the bump on her forehead. All this she could deal with. After all, she had been caught in the head in the martial arts ring several times, but afterwards you always had time to recover, to sit there without having to do anything. Right now, she needed to get back on to work.

Richard appeared again in the room with another cup of tea. Kirsten slapped the bed, indicating he should sit beside her. The strong man took up his place and the two of them sat staring across the room. It was seven in the morning and

Kirsten wondered if she had dozed at some point.

'Why are we doing this? Why isn't it just all hands to the pump looking for this guy? Why has it been done so quietly?'

'Anna wants promotion. You've not worked that out yet?' said Richard.

'Promotion? We've got a potential killer on the loose. Somebody's performing a hit in whatever shape or fashion, it's somebody well-known and she wants promotion?'

'Of course she does. She's done this all in the dark. It's just you. You're just in the door, so, if this all comes off, people will say, 'Yeah, Kirsten did well, but Anna was handling her. Anna was the brains above it.' She wants to go up the ranks. That's all Anna's about. Be careful what she does with you. I've been bitten a few times. She'd happily sacrifice a pawn to get up there. Why do you think I do her bodyguard duty? I dropped out of field ops. Field ops with Anna is nothing to write home about.'

'But we've got to put it on me. I need to put things right. I mean, the guy could be anywhere in Scotland. He could be doing anything.'

'But it's likely to be up in the highlands, isn't it?' said Richard. 'Think about it. Driving all the way up from London to here—why? To pop him back to Glasgow? No, you wouldn't do that. You'd take him out west towards Stranraer. You'd take him into the borders, hide him in there. Plenty of places to go hide without having to travel all the way up here.'

'But you could raid the brothel,' said Kirsten.

'No, she could drop that. That's not important. You realise that, don't you?'

'I had guys look at me. I'm sure she was trying to identify me. Nobody could.'

'And that's why Anna wanted you in there, fresh face. It gets harder the more you do field ops, especially in a small locale. Certain people, they start to recognize you. That's another reason why I'm not out there, but no matter what she says, you've done well, Kirsten. You've done good. You've given us a chance at finding this guy.'

'What's she going to do about it?'

'Well, the police are all onto it, but she'll spin it. Police have been looking for the person that killed two people last night by the camper van. She'll get a foot in there, things will be changed. The story will be, they're looking for this guy. The camper van suspects will be people coming to chase you, either that or a serious bust up will be spun for the police. They'll have to give a line so the public doesn't panic. Then there'll be the murder team investigating as usual.'

Kirsten suddenly slumped in the bed. 'Macleod, Hope McGrath, Ross, they'll all be there, looking at these bodies wondering what's up? Will it stop them investigating?'

'They will get directed,' said Richard. 'They'll get there, they'll pull up forensics; if anything is found, it will be passed upstairs or cut from under them, made known that they don't need to delve too deep. They'll explain that you acted in self-defence, but because of the Official Secrets Act, they can't mention it. They can't mention what you're doing. Bigger fish to fry and all that. You must have got that sometimes when you were on the murder team.'

'I was never in charge though,' said Kirsten. 'The boss wouldn't share something like that. He'd be much more professional than I would.'

'Well, in the meantime, get some more rest. I wouldn't do anything until she calls you and asks you to. Certainly, if you've got any ideas of your own, I'd run it past her first. That's the thing about Anna; she is not that boss who won't go for things, but you need to steer her, you need to be on top. Otherwise, she'll happily toss you into a deadly situation. You don't get away from many of those, Kirsten. You got away from one last night. Try not put yourself in that situation.'

Richard smiled, slapped Kirsten on the thigh, stood up and disappeared back downstairs. Kirsten got up and went for a proper shower and when she came out, she found Richard had left some clothing at the side of the bed. Popping on some jeans and a T-shirt, she made her way downstairs, to find Richard on the phone. When Kirsten went to interrupt him, he held up his hand and kept grunting as if being fed information.

'Yes, I'll get her to it, not to worry.'

When the receiver down, Richard looked up at Kirsten, shaking his head.

'What's up?'

'Your man works fast, as do we. Unfortunately, they're working too fast. A police officer thought he saw someone up near Dornoch following your description being put out on general alert. He saw the driver of a car who fitted the description and followed the car to a chalet. He was told to wait but said that the suspect looked like they weren't staying long, so he went in to have a look. There's a dead body up at that holiday site, now. She wants you to go up, see if you can find anything. See where he might have moved on, see if the man set up but had to run quick.'

'Did they say what happened to the officer?'

'Two shots in the head, face on. Looks like a professional. I reckon it is your man because very few people shoot police officers straight in the face,' said Richard.

173

'I'll get up and get on then. Have you got a car anywhere?'

'You can drop me off and take the one outside. Not my car anyway.'

Kirsten followed Richard outside, got behind the wheel, and and dropped him off at a bus stop. After passing a service station and picking up a coffee and a bacon roll, she continued to drive up towards Dornoch. At the side of one of the main roads, sat a small holiday park with about eight chalets. Around one of them was a large screen.

A number of police cars were sitting with flashing lights, as well as a couple of unmarked cars at the rear. Kirsten parked her car just beyond and started to walk down towards the scene. As she got closer, she saw a face she knew sitting in a car. DC Alan Ross was checking through his laptop when she rapped on his window. He turned, smiled, and pressed the button for the window to descend.

'Kirsten. What on earth, Kirsten? Hasn't got too much for you already, has it?'

'Alan Ross, how you coping without me? You doing all the spade work?'

'No,' he said. 'There's a new Sergeant. Clarissa Urquhart. There at the far end. She gives the boss a run for his money but I'm guessing you're here for a reason. You haven't just popped by for a busman's holiday, have you?'

'No,' said Kirsten, 'and I can't say why I'm here either, other than, yes, there's a dead body in there, but you probably worked that bit out for yourself.'

'I did, but look at that knock on your head. You've been in the wars.'

'More than you know,' she said. Inside, Kirsten could feel tears coming. Ross had been a good friend and with what had happened the previous evening, she wanted to sit down beside him, tell him, let the tears flow but she knew she couldn't. She had to operate completely in the dark.

'I'll just go see the old man.'

'Don't let them hear you call him that. He's always paranoid about his age and the young bucks coming behind him. You know that.'

'Yes, but you got to keep him on his toes,' laughed Kirsten, but she didn't really feel like it. She was exhausted, tired, and those faces were still coming.

Detective Inspector Macleod wore a dark suit with a black tie. He had a small hat on his head and his face was perplexed as he stood looking into the chalet at the centre of the incident. Kirsten stepped onto the gravel path towards the chalet and the man spun his head around.

'Stewart, imagine that, you here.'

'You don't sound particularly surprised, sir.'

'You don't have to call me sir. Well, you didn't have to call me sir back then either but you certainly don't have to now. Seoras, it's Seoras, Kirsten.'

'No. It's always sir or the inspector. You'll never be Seoras.'

'It is my name,' he laughed, 'but I did think you'd be here.'

'Why?' asked Kirsten. Macleod moved closer and leaned in beside her.

'Two shots straight to the head, police officer. Didn't bat an eye. Not a normal criminal. You got a hitman on the list?'

Kirsten had to fight hard not to react. 'We are just continuing our own inquiries.'

'You better get him off the streets soon. What's the deal then?'

'The deal is I don't answer. You know that.'

'I haven't got any word,' said Macleod. 'If it's that sort of a case, I get word from above. Otherwise, I've got to investigate this fully, you know.'

'Has your boss not dropped word in? No instructions?'

'No,' said Macleod, 'but I don't fancy sending my people after this one either. You get too close with these ones and it's bang and you're dead. He hasn't argued, no questions. The officer hasn't even made it inside. He's come to the door looking for trouble.'

'What did the records say about the officer? Had he checked in at all to say he was popping in?'

'He called on the radio about the suspect, said he'd seen him. He was told that we were only to follow, but nobody said it was this dangerous. Nobody said, hitman. What's going on, Kirsten?'

'I can't say, inspector. We don't work that way anymore, not on this job.'

'Well, you chose it.'

You encouraged me, thought Kirsten. *You said I'd be good at it. You said I was right for it, but you didn't tell me I'd have to kill people. You didn't tell me that sometimes it goes wrong.*

'Is everything going well?' asked Macleod.

'Perfect,' said Kirsten. 'Just perfect.'

'Liar,' said Macleod. 'You're a liar, but that's your job now, isn't it?' He turned, put his arms on her shoulders, and looked into her eyes. 'Whatever it is that's happened, it won't be your fault. You do what you're meant to do. You're too solid to make bad mistakes.' Kirsten wanted to step away, out of his gaze, either to tell him everything or to run and hide because she knew she could not. Macleod was always sharp. He could read people, situations, but at the moment he was angry because there were murders in his patch that he did not have the whole information for.

'Is this one linked to the dead guys at the camper van?' asked Macleod. 'Because we're kind of busy this morning.'

Kirsten looked around and saw Hope McGrath was not there. 'Yes,' said Macleod. 'She's back there looking after that one. That other one was pretty nasty. Good shots as well. Two to the head, but you know what, Kirsten? They weren't as good as this. These shots were brutally good. These came from an experienced hand. I'd have said the other one was from an inexperienced hand, albeit, shot well.'

Stewart looked up. *Somebody must've told him, surely*.

'Oh, sorry,' said Macleod. 'You shouldn't have to do that. Though, I'm sure you did it with the very best of reasons.'

'I'm just going to have a look around this stuff, if it's all right with you, inspector.'

'Of course, but don't touch anything, or put gloves on if you do. Jona will have you.' Jona Nakamura was the main forensic investigator in Inverness.

Kirsten stepped inside the chalet, but as much as she looked, she could not see anything out of place. There was a list detailing everything in the chalet, and Kirsten went through it and found nothing extra.

'Is that everything?' asked Kirsten on her way out the door.

Macleod looked over, 'What do you mean, is that everything? You looking for something in particular?'

'Yes, especially anything with a time or date.'

'Well,' said Macleod, 'I wish you'd said earlier because Jona got something. Pen and paper were left behind within, but she did the old trick of just running a pencil across it. Sure enough, there was an impression made.'

'I better go and see her then,' said Kirsten.

'I hope you get better,' said Macleod.

Kirsten watched his eyes on her as she walked away. Then she stopped.

'Thank you, inspector. See you around.'

'Get it seen to,' said Macleod. 'Whatever it is, get it seen to.'

Chapter 21

J ona Nakamura was the Chief Forensic Officer at
Inverness Police Station and someone Kirsten Stewart
had worked with before. Generally, she would have seen
her for routine things, picking up reports, and turning in
evidence. Kirsten always used to find the diminutive Asian
woman to be a little aloof when it came to their relationship.
However, the pair of women were of equal height, Jona,
quite slim and petite, whilst Kirsten was more rounded and
muscular due to the mixed martial arts she had been heavily
involved in. But Kirsten was under no doubt about Jona
Nakamura's qualifications and ability to hunt down things
from a forensic aspect.

The small wagon that served as a mobile operations base for
the forensic unit was along from the chalet where the police
officer had been shot dead. As Kirsten approached, a police
officer raised his hand stopping her in her tracks.

'I'm afraid this is off-limits, ma'am. We don't want the public
in here.'

'Quite right, officer, you don't. Could you possibly pass a
message through to Ms. Nakamura in the back?' The officer
looked at Kirsten, surprised she would know the woman's

name. 'If you can just tell Jona that an old friend is sitting outside and could do with a word.'

'I'm afraid Ms. Nakamura is actually on a case at the moment. I doubt she would have time for that sort of thing. Are you press?'

'I'm not press and I've just come from speaking to the Detective Inspector over there. If you want, I'll go back, bring him over so he can point out the fact that he told me to go see Jona.'

'Just a second,' said the officer. He clearly was not crazy and the idea of incurring Macleod's wrath was not one anyone would want to entertain, ever. Still, he was not just going to let anyone walk into a forensic mobile laboratory.

The officer returned two minutes later, apologised, and said that Ms. Nakamura would be out in a few moments. When she did, the Asian woman looked tense as if the weight of a world was on her shoulders.

'Jona,' said Kirsten. 'It's good to see you again.' There was a sudden splash of realisation across Jona's face and she waved Kirsten over and took her around the side of the forensic wagon.

'It is one of those, is it?' said Jona. 'Surprised we haven't had a tight lip order slapped on us.'

'I'm surprised as well,' said Kirsten. 'The inspector said that you would have something for me. He said you discovered something written down. A time?'

'Yes,' said Jona, and pulled out a mobile phone, opening up the picture gallery. 'If you look here, the pad of paper was written on and then the top was torn off. We've got a slightly fancier fashion but if you scrub the pencil across it, you basically will get this.'

Kirsten looked at the picture; '25th!' she said. 'That's like, yes, tomorrow. 25th, 2:30 p.m. It didn't have anything else with it?' asked Kirsten.

'No, nothing else written on the card, just that. Is it important?' asked Jona.

'I'd say that could be very important,' replied Kirsten. 'I don't know why; I don't know—well, actually,' she said, 'that would be a lie. I do have a good idea why. I can't tell you, but this one, I hope has no end. Thank you, Jona. Helpful as ever.' Kirsten shook her hand.

'I didn't ask where I should send all the rest of the reports to.'

'Not me,' said Kirsten. 'I do as I'm told, very much like yourself.'

'That much hasn't changed.'

As Kirsten walked off, she glanced back over towards the chalet, where she saw Macleod pondering the distant skyline. He was always like that, little action and more a bucket of thought. Though you couldn't blame him, the age he was getting to. She always felt that's why he liked her around him. She could handle herself, but then so could his Sergeant Hope McGrath.

Kirsten made her way back to Inverness. Having reached her own office, she sat down behind her laptop and began to check through engagements or other public events happening the next day. It took an hour to troll through the internet. On the pad of paper beside her, Kirsten had three specific targets.

A prominent scientist was coming to the University. This was quite a big deal and the University had laid on the works. The trouble with the scientist was, he was a large supporter of the government, and that's what made Kirsten think he could be a potential target.

The Chief Constable also had a public meeting, but that would be carried out in the steps of a Law Court in Glasgow. Still, you couldn't overlook it. There was also a TV star starting a charity auction exactly at 2:30 p.m. in the large park in Inverness. There would be a large stage built, music, a large crowd as well, and the potential for a statement. The TV star was Asian, and had been a large supporter of the rights of refugees and immigrants, especially from the far east coming to the country.

However, Kirsten found these particular targets problematic. If he shot the scientist, why? He was prominent in the scientific community but not that well known beyond. The Chief Constable was there whoever was in power, so it wasn't really a political statement. The Constable's own particular views on the current politicians were not well known, although like every current Constable, he kept on harping on about resources, about how the current government wasn't giving enough. She thought, *Not an ideal candidate*.

The last one, the TV star, would surely send the wrong message. Although popular, the person was not in government. TV stars were not the ones who actually made any decisions; could you blame them for sticking up for the rights of their own people? Just an awkward target to take out in such a way. However, these were the only targets that Stewart could come up with. She picked up the phone to Anna Hunt and was pleasantly surprised to find that she answered instead of Richard.

'You come back out of the woodwork then? I hope you've got me back on the trail here.'

'The shooting up at Dornoch was definitely our man. Very

professional hit on the police officer, but he's been forced to move on. We did find a message left behind left on a part on paper—just a date and a time: the 25th, 2:30 p.m.'

'But that's tomorrow.'

'Yes,' said Kirsten, 'I'm well aware of that. I've checked tomorrow's schedules. At 2:30 p.m., the only thing I can see is the scientist opening up the new wing at the university. The Chief Constable will be down in Glasgow at a reception—he'd be on the steps of one of the lower courts; and we've got that TV star from Asia, the one that kicks up for human rights doing a concert in the park in Inverness.'

'And you think it's any of those?'

'I don't think it's anything,' said Stewart. 'I don't agree with this. It's too easy, too simple. You won't get sympathy for shooting a TV star. Chief Constable is apolitical. On the scientist, it just doesn't feel like a big enough target. They brought over a specialist from a foreign country. They've been prepared to kill, to keep it a secret. They were taking me off the street to use me and then dispose of me. There's something else going on, something else.'

'I take it you checked up on the political parties.'

'Well, they're only against the government. I doubt they'll take a hit on any of the opposition. The first minister is not here. She hasn't got a schedule for anything, nothing official. So, unless they're getting insider knowledge of her personal habits, I don't think it's going to be on her. It wouldn't be a public statement anyway if they were to shoot her in private. It'll just look like a killing and that's not what they want. There is a political thing behind this, as much as they're working with a gang of bandits to do it.'

'I think it's time for us to come into the light, Kirsten. I'm going to organize cover on all of this. You've done a good job, so time for you to take a break. I'm going to get sorted here, make sure I've got people at all these occasions. It's going to be one of them. There's nothing else you say, even in the afternoon.'

'Nothing I can pinpoint,' said Kirsten, 'but you feel free to go over it.'

'Well, you've given us a chance, Kirsten. You may have lost him in the first place or at least could have killed him but we probably know where he's going. As I said, stand down. You've worked hard the last couple of days, and Richard said you were struggling. It's not easy to take out people. I remember my first one. When you see what these bastards can do, you'll learn to get past that.'

Kirsten always thought Anna Hunt was harsh, but then maybe she had just seen more than Kirsten. It was very different when someone was after you, ready to kill you—even worse when they were ready to dispose of a woman who had nothing to do with either of them.

Kirsten put the phone down, closed her laptop, and prepared to take herself home. Home, as she called it, was the centre where she kept her brother, where would she go alone this afternoon, to sit and watch him. He would not know who she was, but at least she would get him when he was up and about, could still see him interacting with people. She might even be lucky and be able to give him a drink or something. Although often he would get agitated if he didn't know who was serving him. It was such a shame of her brother but then she had never known him to not have difficulties.

When their parents had died, they were both young. They'd grown up through a foster family, but Kirsten had taken him on board as soon as she was legally able to and she was glad she had done it.

She should probably also go and see a doctor, one from the service, of course, to get her head seen to. Also get a shrink because she was sure that these killings were going to come back at her.

Kirsten made her way down the stairs and hopped on a bus in Inverness Town Centre. From there, she would hop on another one which would take her right to her brother's but when she arrived in the centre of town, she simply got off and began to wander. For the next hour, Kirsten stood in front of clothes, lifting them, looking at them, wondering if they fit, and putting them back, but her mind was going overtime. When she sat down for a coffee, she did not even notice the person waving at her, explaining that she had forgotten to take the cup down to the table. Something was playing on her mind and Kirsten needed to work out what it was.

This job was not finished. This was not what was going to happen. These three incidents don't fit. Kirsten thought about what Richard had said about Anna Hunt off looking for the glory, now having sidelined Kirsten. Kirsten didn't care about the glory. All she cared about was the fact that the three targets they had come up with did not seem to be highly realistic.

Kirsten picked out her mobile, a spare one that she kept back at the office and brought with her. One day, she would drive to Fort William and pick up the other one, just as soon as this was over. She rang a number she knew well.

'Macleod.'

'Inspector, it's Kirsten.'

'Twice in one day? Do you want me to come and solve the thing for you?'

'Not necessary. I've got an issue. The boss thinks that something's going to happen, and she's tightened it down to three different options. She's moved me off it and gone to organize cover for it all, run the operation herself.'

'And? That's her prerogative. You've done a lot of work, presumably. Take your time off.'

'That's the problem, Seoras, I can't. I don't think she's right. I mean, I don't think I'm right.'

'You're not making sense now,' said Macleod.

'I came up with these targets for her and they fit a time and a place, but I don't think I'm right.'

'Targets?' said Macleod. Kirsten realised she had dropped a clanger. It was one thing to talk about decisions and keep them theoretical. Without names or actual places to them but she had said the word *target*. Macleod had come from presumably seeing a hitman kill a police officer, so the word target was highly provocative.

'You don't believe she's got this right, but you've got it right?'

'No, but I'm off the case. I'm told to rest.'

'Do you remember,' said Macleod, 'Fort Augustus?'

Kirsten struggled to forget Fort Augustus. As a team they had been following an individual who had committed several terrorist-type acts along the west coast. While everyone else had thought it was a terrorist, Macleod and the team had narrowed it down to an individual, but the last act of the individual was taking place in Fort Augustus. Kirsten Stewart, Sergeant Hope McGrath, and DC Ross were struggling to get there on time. The detective inspector was sitting in Inverness Hospital, where his partner's life was on the line. The inspector had come, prevented the last attack, and then simply returned.

'There is no off-duty,' said Macleod. 'We're always on duty, and if you think something isn't right, you go and find it. If you have to do it in the dark, you find out what's right and then work out how to bring it to the light.'

'I haven't really got the authority to keep going. I could screw this up. I could warn them by doing that.'

'They didn't want you to go and be a little robot,' said Macleod. 'They took you because you're Kirsten Stewart. I brought you on my team because you were Kirsten Stewart. I want Kirsten Stewart, the clever woman who can work things out, but also the woman who stood and defended me in Barra.'

Kirsten remembered the street fight she had got into.

'You're there to protect, Kirsten. Go and protect. People's lives are in danger. Go solve it. It's what we do. You don't need any instruction to do that, do you?'

Kirsten realised what Macleod was saying. To hell with Anna Hunt, Kirsten would have to go and solve this. She had to find where this killer was.

'Thank you, Inspector,' said Kirsten and then closed the call.

Chapter 22

Kirsten needed a way in, a way to check where everyone was. She had already looked up the official dates put in for the first minister of Scotland and also for the Royal Family. She could not connect the time and date to any particular event. *What if it wasn't a public event? What if it was a private one, something else?* She did not get told when these dates were, and if she went looking for them, Anna Hunt would know she was cutting around the back. Kirsten pondered what to do and then called into the main office, hoping to find someone there. When a voice answered the phone, she knew she was in luck.

Justin Chivers, because he was a computer expert, generally got left out off the main operations. He analysed, dug deep into accounts and other computer based details. He was certainly no man of action. He may have thought himself one and also God's gift to women, but he was not. Kirsten saw Justin more as a guy who would sit eating a packet of potato crisps watching late-night television. She thought Justin would be lucky to find the door rather than the great outdoors.

'Justin, anyone else about?'

'No. I hear you've been making trouble. I hope you're still

intact. I'd hate to see any bit of you get injured.'

Kirsten could feel the slime coming from the remarks. Justin knew exactly how to cut it fine. He had been brought up on disciplinary twice before within the service for making sexist remarks. Once, he had been accused of trying to have a fumble with one of the secretaries and sported a shiner that day, but even that had failed to get him kicked out. The reason was he was just too darn good at what he did and so they had slapped restraining orders on him, made sure certain office staff never saw him, but unfortunately, Kirsten needed him right now.

'Yes, I'm intact. I'm okay, Justin, but thank you for asking,' said Kirsten in a patronising tone. 'It's what happens to us who work outside, but I need you now.'

'Ooh, that sounds promising,' said Justin.

Kirsten ignored the comment. 'I've got a date and time: 25th, 2:30 p.m. I'd like you to find out for me where each of the royals is going to be. Also, the first minister, the deputy first minister, and anyone else that's high up within government.'

'Why? Anna Hunt's afoot organising three different sets of teams to cover events. I thought you'd find which one they were going for.'

'Let's just say I'm keeping the cards close to my chest.'

When she said the word, Kirsten thought she heard the man almost dribble. He was pathetic. She made a mental note to appear in the most frumpy-looking thing possible the next time she saw him.

'Look, Justin, just get on with it. Punch me through whatever answers you come up with.'

'Why can't you do it? Just go and ask for it.'

'Sidelined. Meant to be resting with trauma and that. Anna's got my best interests at heart, but I have to be sure of this. Can you do that for me?'

'For you, I would do anything,' said Justin. Kirsten felt a shiver in her spine. He was so creepy.

Knowing that Justin would come through, Kirsten decided to take a few minutes and put her feet up at the coffee house. Again, she felt numb, her mind casting back to the night before. She could still see the face of the dead men. Well, what remained of one of them. Then she thought about Macleod. He was slightly aloof for someone who had always supported her, thought so well of her. Maybe he was doing that because he could not know what she was about. She understood that whenever he was being a gentleman and not trying to put her under any pressure to reveal secrets, she should not. Kirsten suddenly thought it best not to think about this, not to think about her former boss and to just get on with what was occurring. It took another twenty-five minutes before Justin Chivers called back.

'You're going to owe me for this one,' he said.

'Why?'

'Because I had to call in some pretty big favours. You're asking me to find out where the royals are. They don't just fire out her private arrangements on a canteen noticeboard.'

'No, but we're here to protect.'

'And I am a lonely operative, not a section head. What I found out is, Her Majesty's down in England. It looks like she's on her own time at the castle.' Justin was referring to Buckingham Palace but he always called it 'the castle' for some reason. He certainly was not a royalist.

'Struggling to find out if the rest of the royals could be any sort of target. Well, they have a speech being made by the queen's daughter. However, that's on the south coast. The rest of them aren't in Scotland. Deputy first minister is chairing a committee tomorrow. It's inside Holyrood. Certainly, no public occasion, hard to get at.'

'What about the first minister? Where will she be?'

'Apparently, on a private arrangement. It looks like the Earl of Dunblane is having her over to his place. Few others involved but yes, it's quite out of the way though in the Cairngorms.'

'So, it's within range? A hitman would come to Inverness, not stop in Glasgow,' said Kirsten.

'That's true but it's really quite well protected. She's inside almost a castle-like structure.'

'What's the address?' asked Kirsten.

Justin passed on the detail. Kirsten realised that she would be almost twenty miles south of Aviemore, up in the hills. The building was a castle but a small one that had been converted recently. There were many modern parts to it, built on against conservationists' wishes, but that was progress.

'Thanks, Justin. I'd say I owe you one, but I know the sort of favour you'd look for.'

'Well, you know me that well. Anytime you want, I can fulfil that.'

'Bye, Justin. Thank you for your help.' Kirsten put the phone down and then looked around for car keys. Of course, her own car was still down in Fort William. She jumped on the bus, went into town, and picked up a hire car. Kirsten made her way along the A9 to the Cairngorms. Once she was about twenty miles south of Aviemore, she turned off the A9, cutting up into the mountains. The castle was on the side of one of the smaller mountains but was located in a valley well off the main Inverness to Perth road. You couldn't see it from the

191

road.

Having to travel up there, Kirsten drove along the entrance to the estate. She could see there was already security there, but it wasn't government security. Maybe they had appeared earlier on in the week. She thought that was the standard protocol, making sure everything was okay for the first minister. Kirsten drove along around the estate, looking at the castle through binoculars, every now and again when she stopped.

The building was pretty self-contained. If you were going to kill someone, you'd have to get inside the building. For that, she would have to trust the security. She had no reason to believe that they would not be up to the task. It would be quite something for a killer to breach those gates and get all the way in, dispatching people. It did not seem reasonable.

As far as she could tell, there was a small veranda at the rear that the first minister would be unlikely to use due to the openness to the countryside. Otherwise, the location was perfect. She would be inside and out of sight the whole time. Maybe Kirsten had drawn a blank and she started to make her way back up the A9 towards Inverness again. As she drove along, her mobile beeped. She pulled over into a lay-by. Taking it out, she saw a missed call and message from Justin Chivers.

'Looked into the first minister's visit for you, to the Earl of Dunblane's. There was a guest list, a private one that's been published for department eyes only and without its section heads. I've got friends who can get me these things.'

Kirsten understood that this didn't mean friends had acquired it for him, but rather, Chivers was capable of breaking into the system. He would of course do it in such a way not to bring attention to himself. This piece of paper was fairly low key.

'I'll text it over to you. Keep it all safe for me. I wouldn't like to see that little body of yours getting injured.'

He made Kirsten sick with his little comments about her body. He had mentioned it more often than her doctor did, and at least Doctor Graham was doing it for medical reasons. Kirsten looked down at the phone and saw the email had arrived with the guest list on it. Maybe she was taking this too far. It all seemed a bit ridiculous now having seen the site, but she decided to open the email anyway and have a look.

Scrolling down the names, Kirsten wondered why this was not an official event. Then she realised it was more to do with the party, not the government. The first minister, although in charge of the country, was also heavily involved in party duties and, obviously, the Earl of Dunblane was providing a venue for her to conduct some party business.

This rang a bell in Kirsten's head. The group that was looking to carry this out was doing it to upset the government, and here was someone sponsoring the government to work out their own plans. This wasn't anything to do with the country. This was to do with staying in power, and that could be a potential target. What a statement that would make for a first minister to be found dead amongst people who were looking to plot their own self-interests, persuade the government for their own ends.

Kirsten began scanning the list. She did not know most of the people, but she opened up her laptop and started looking them up. They were indeed members of the party. Some very small fry, others bigger. A couple of the ministers of government were there as well but in their party capacity. *There will be a lot of security around it, so how on earth was this guy going to take her out if she was the target, or were they all the target?*

Maybe he had planted a bomb. If he did, it would be up to the forces already employed to protect to find it. There was no way Kirsten could search for that sort of thing. As her fingers scanned down, she continued to look through the people who were coming. The joy of the Internet was most people had a picture of their face somewhere, especially if you were of any sort of prominence at all. Although she did not know the names, she did check the faces, and none of them rang a bell to her.

One of the last names on the list was described as a guide for the first minister. Apparently, she had asked for a tour of the castle, and someone had been specifically chosen. His name, Arthur Mackenzie, brought up a lot of faces in the search, but none of them seemed to be related to what Kirsten was investigating. Surely, to get into position like that, they would have to be known somewhere. Kirsten scrolled through the photos taken from other articles across the world wide web.

It was on the third page that something struck her as strange. She was looking at a face that she had seen before. She couldn't remember where. The face itself was in some ways very nondescript, but the eyes said something different to her. In her training, Kirsten had been taught to recognise things and hold them in memory. Now, she closed her own eyes trying to reconjure that face. *Where had she seen the eyes?* Then it dawned on her.

When she was back in the room in Fort William listening to the colonel speak, she had seen that face. It was the colonel up on stage, except he had hair in this picture. It also didn't say Arthur Mackenzie, it was Art Mack he was known as, a shortened form. Kirsten re-entered the search title as Art Mack, and two more photographs came up with the same person. Archaeological guide for hire, said one underneath. Another was a small article talking about castles written by Art Mack with a photo of himself at the bottom. Clearly, Arthur Mackenzie, aka the colonel, had the ability to be a guide. *Was this his cover? Why was he there? His politics were certainly not in the right place. It couldn't be a coincidence, could it?*

Kirsten looked at the photograph. The eyes were the same. The hair was different and the face, puffier. It was like there was more fat on the cheekbones, more to the nose. *Was this the same person?*

Kirsten sat back, closed her eyes, and tried to think. If she went ahead with this and it was wrong, she would be kicking up trouble for herself. However, if she left it, no one would know, but someone could be dead. 'You have to protect,' Macleod had said. 'That's what we do.' *I need to follow that*, she thought. Picking up her mobile, she tapped in the number for Anna Hunt.

Chapter 23

Anna Hunt was not on the end of the phone. Instead Richard Lafferty answered.

'She does not want to be disturbed. She's in conference at the moment making plans for these other three sites. I don't think she's going to go for this, Kirsten. She's got a whole force behind her here. She had to go and get some ministerial approval for the firepower she's brought in. Double security here, there, and everywhere. She's not going to be keen to hear another solution.'

'But this one makes more sense,' said Kirsten, 'and I think there's somebody on the inside.'

'I'll go and get her if you're insistent,' said Richard, 'but I'm just warning you, you better sell it good.'

Kirsten held on the phone for ten minutes before Anna Hunt arrived. She was not best pleased.

'Why are you trying to tell me of a different target?'

'I warned you before. I said I wasn't convinced on the other three.'

'And you're more convinced on this? On what? How is the timing working? How is the date? The first minister's at a private function. It's got nothing to do with government, it's

196

just her party. Nobody will see it.'

'It's the first minister, nobody has to see it. It just has to be done. Make your statement afterwards.'

'But the others are much more public. That's what you said, they wanted to make a point.'

'But the point made with the first minister is not the same as making a point with some random scientist or chief constable. No, this is different. Besides, I believe there's someone on the inside.'

'Someone on the inside? Are you sure?'

'I think it's the colonel I saw in Fort William. At least it certainly has a resemblance to him. Arthur Mackenzie on the list. He's meant to be showing the first minister the history of the castle. He's an expert, has papers up and other written pieces, but when I look at him, I swear it's the same person. The time could be just an agreed time to bring her to an open shot.'

'But that's up at the Earl of Dunblane's, isn't it? It's the Earl of Dunblane's place. He's sound. Totally sound. I'll ring them for you when I get a chance, but that's it. Take no further action. You're meant to be off the job, so enough. Sit this one out. We've got it covered.'

'Let me know what you think, though.'

'I mean it, Kirsten. You sit this one out. You have done plenty. There's enough of you in the report. You've come in at the bottom and you've made an impact. Go and take some time. Richard said you were pretty cut up over those two goons you put down. Go and see the doctor. Sort it out. Make sure you're up and ready for the next one. I'll be busy so don't bother me. I'll come to you if I think it's worthwhile.'

Stewart was disgusted as she put the phone down and began

to walk along the side of the mountain that looked onto the castle. She could see a veranda at the side, a perfect place to shoot at, but the first minister was unlikely to come out there. They would know that.

Ahead of her, water cascaded down from high above. For a moment, Kirsten took in the breath-taking view. She could feel the spray floating across to her and she closed her eyes, letting it soothe her face. She breathed in deeply, smelling the freshness. There was something cleaner about the air up here. Inverness, whilst being a city, was far less crowded than many others, but even so, it didn't compare to being out in the open.

Kirsten looked around her. If I would shoot, where would I shoot from? You can hide in the grass here, but nobody would, too easy to spot. If the first minister was coming up, this mountain side would be pored over, probably tomorrow morning. They would have done a cursory check already, picked out places that could be a danger.

Kirsten looked around and wondered where else a person could hide. There did not seem to be anywhere. Slowly, she walked back to the car, got inside, and drove back to Inverness. It could be tomorrow's problem. After all, that was the date and the time, tomorrow afternoon and the first minister wasn't there yet. For once, it couldn't happen tonight.

Inside her flat, Kirsten put her feet up on the bed and watched something on TV. She could not quite work out what it was, but then again, she was not paying any attention. It seemed to be some sort of soap, but there was a comedy element to it that she could not quite grasp. Maybe it was an American thing—they did not always carry over. That's what got her. They spoke roughly the same language, had come in history from roughly the same place and yet nowadays, the

United Kingdom and America were so very different.

Kirsten was unusual in the sense she carried a gun. The normal police did not. They may have had special response squads who were weaponised, but most people were not, and even in her capacity working for the secret services, she did not carry a gun all the time. They were often loud and even with a silencer they still made a noise. Kirsten had been taught how to take people out without making a sound, much more effective and easier to control, people had said. Kirsten agreed, though she did not like the idea of taking anyone out whatever had happened.

By ten o'clock the next morning, Kirsten was back in the Cairngorms. She had not heard anything from Anna Hunt, and she doubted she would. The woman was dismissive of her claims, and yet Kirsten couldn't get the eyes out of her head. She called in to Jason Chivers who offered some incredibly rude comment, but agreed to Kirsten's request to trial a face match from her description to that of Arthur Mackenzie. It was a long shot, because he would have to draw up a photo fit from Kirsten's description and then match it to the real person. It was unlikely, to say the least.

When Jason phoned back just before midday, the match had said thirty percent. There was no point phoning straight to Anna, she would not have gone with that, and anyway, the first minister was already here. Kirsten had stayed up on the road, high above the castle. From there she looked like a tourist simply looking around, but she did note the men walking back and forward across the mountainside searching, making sure everything was clear.

Kirsten sat on the car bonnet with a pair of binoculars, looking as if she was just enjoying the view, but instead she was scanning every boulder. It was crazy, there was an entire detachment of people doing this, but still Kirsten persisted though her latest scan produced nothing. She went inside the car to get a packet of sandwiches she had bought at a local supermarket and opened up the fizzy juice that came with it. She chewed her morsels of food slowly, washing them down a piece at a time. Kirsten never ate properly when her mind was occupied, and the problem at the moment was there was more than one thing occupying it.

The previous night's sleep had been fitful. Once again, she'd seen faces of dead men, faces that had been blown away, or double marked with shots through the head. She had woken up at four o'clock, sweating profusely, so much so that she had got out of bed and taken a shower before returning. She had wondered what it would have been like to have someone in the bed beside her, someone who could have empathised even if he didn't understand. He could have rubbed her back, shoulders, relaxed her muscles, maybe even taken some of the frustration out through sex.

Kirsten had never been good at the relationship side. Having a brother had seen to that. Her brother needed so much care and attention so there was only the odd night, but few and far between, and if she was honest, she regretted it.

Kirsten didn't move from her car. She was well aware that if she started to move into a dangerous position, one they considered a place to be able to shoot at the castle from people will converge, check out what she was doing.

Two o'clock came and went. For all Kirsten knew, everything inside the castle was just as planned. Nobody had come out onto the veranda and still, people had strode back and forward across the valley below and on the hillside across, some with weapons far greater than Kirsten's. Still, she had come armed.

Then again, maybe this was all a wild goose chase. Maybe she would sit here, get to five o'clock, get in her car, and drive home to an empty bed. Or home to see her brother. She would certainly do that, see her brother when this was all done. Anna had gone on about getting her head sorted, so maybe two weeks' leave was worth taking. She could get it on the sick as well. That would be better.

But at the back of Kirsten's mind was Macleod's voice, 'We protect.' That's why she was here, to protect, but where was the danger? Where had it gone, and who else would be in trouble if this wasn't the place? No reports had come through of anything found at the other three sites Anna Hunt was covering. Although Kirsten was meant to be off duty and would not receive any instant updates, she had asked Richard to message her when possible if anything had turned up. He had taken the request kindly, but the man was busy. Covering three sites at once was not easy for any person and his boss was making full use of him.

It was 2:25 p.m. when Kirsten spotted somebody on the veranda. She took out her binoculars but was struggling to make out exactly who it was. However, several other people followed and chairs were placed. When a table was brought out and drinks laid upon it, Kirsten knew something was up. So, they were going to the veranda. After all was said and done, they were coming. A number of people lined the valley below the castle, looking up into the hillside and then back towards the castle as if someone was going to appear magically. They had swept here and there. Kirsten had also brought out her OS map that showed the ground and the contours, but there was nothing. Where would such a lithe and well-toned man go? How could he get away? That was the other issue. You are on the hillside with everybody watching. You would need to be able to shoot from a place that would allow you to run. As soon as you did, people would shoot back.

Think, Kirsten, think, she said to herself. Looking down through the binoculars at the veranda, it could only be a couple of minutes before the first minister would come out. The hillside was covered, but if they had put a helicopter over, which no doubt they would have done, you would see the heat signature of someone lying low, even if they were covered up in mud. Even if they disguised their heat, the ground had been so trampled. *Where would you go after you did the shot? You'd surely be picked out quickly.*

Kirsten looked down at her map again and realised some-thing. The map itself showed contour and terrain, but it did not show exactly how things were. Yes, the hillside you could tell from the lines, but there was a waterfall there, a large one at that. It was cut into the hill, and you saw the lines of the contours indicating this, but in front of it was water dropping. You could not look up and spot someone through the water. You could not make the shot through water either, could you? Then again, how much of a shot did you need to do? If the first minister was placed in a certain area, you could spray all around that area and she would be unlikely to survive. Cut her down with a hail of bullets, not one single shot. If you get the right gun and the right position inside the waterfall, it would be so hard to see you.

Would people notice the bullets coming through? Would the force of the water deflect them? Maybe not. Kirsten sighted her binoculars down to the waterfall. Now she looked at it, she realised it was not a constant stream. The water came down but there was plenty of broken bits in between, but nobody would be looking through to the back of it. *Or when you fired a gun, where would the retort go?* The noise would sound like it was across the hillside, not from inside a waterfall.

Through her binoculars, Kirsten saw more people coming out. The waterfall was halfway across the mountain. At the moment, it was maybe a kilometre from her, but if she drove around the top, continued with the road, she could get close. Kirsten put down the binoculars and sped away. Maybe she caused those down below to look up and wonder what this person was doing. Maybe she was becoming a target of interest herself.

With her foot to the floor, she drove just over a kilometre and parked the car at the top of the waterfall. There was a bridge up there and she saw the water flowing underneath. Jumping off the roadside, she started charging through the thick heather and made her way down the side. In one hand, she carried her weapon; in the other was the pair of binoculars.

She stopped quickly, peered at the veranda, and saw the double doors opening at the far side of it. The first minister was starting to come through, being led in discussion by someone. Kirsten took the binoculars from her eyes, quickly striding down the mountainside at the edge of the waterfall. She got close to a point where she lay on her belly, the front half of her almost tumbling over the edge. She could see the water and yet through it, there were gaps, many ledges within that waterfall.

Had he climbed up? If you were a good climber, you could do it. She would have struggled, but if you knew what you were doing and had the right gear . . . She started scanning, getting

203

frustrated by the fact that the waterfall would cut off her vision intermittently. Her eyes struggled to focus back and forward as the water interrupted her scene. Then she saw something. There was a man on a small ledge tucked away. She could just about see his weapon peering out from the front. The man was in a prone position, ready to shoot.

Kirsten saw him adjust, and she reckoned the first minister must nearly be in position. There was a cry above her, someone shouting at her to hold her ground. They had followed her. They had gone to see what she was doing. If they saw the gun, they might shoot. There would be one chance at this, one chance to get this right. Leaning over the edge, Kirsten held her gun in front of her with two hands. She felt herself begin to shake, but drew in a breath, steadying herself. One chance, one chance and make it quick.

'Put the weapon down,' came the shout from up the hill. Kirsten ignored them.

'I said, put the weapon down or I'll shoot.' Kirsten watched the man below adjust his shoulder. He was about to let a hail of bullets rip through the veranda. She fired once, twice, and then a third time. She watched the gun below her fall away, but the man remained in his prone position.

Instinctively, she held her hands up, her own gun now around her thumb.

'Just put that down. Put that down.'

'Kirsten Stewart, special forces. I work for the service. There's a sniper below. Get the first minister inside.'

'Just put the gun down, love.' Kirsten let the gun go to the ground and placed her hands behind her back. Two men quickly arrived to snap cuffs on her before they peered over the side as well.

'Take me in, but that's your killer down there. That was the man ready to kill the first minister.' There was silence from the two men with her, staring down until one of them turned to the other.

'How the hell are we going to get him out of there?'

Chapter 24

Kirsten was taken away to a nearby police station, but once her identity had been confirmed, the handcuffs were released, and apologies were made. She was then led back to the scene where she found a specialist team of mountaineers setting about making their way up the waterfall to recover the body of the shooter. Kirsten made her way back to where she had shot from and realised that she had held steady and shot well. Even now standing and looking over the edge, she felt no wave of emotion, nothing but a good job done.

With the body recovered, the local police station was set up as a hub for the various forces who looked after the protection of the first minister. Kirsten was being debriefed, questioned about who this person was, what he was doing. She advised of the trafficked women, gave the location, and asked that someone be sent soon before they moved. The address in Fort William was also forthcoming, and she envisioned Jock being picked up shortly. Arthur Mackenzie was certainly nabbed.

She had been correct, knowing for sure when she saw him being taken away. Art Mack was indeed the colonel, but there was no smile of indignation, no anger at her. Rather, he simply started to go through his own preaching on how this government had failed. About an hour after returning to the police station for the second time, Kirsten received a call from Anna. The woman was livid. Kirsten could tell, not from what was said to her but rather what was not said. There were no congratulations, no apology for not listening to her. When Richard tried to come on to the call afterwards, he was brutally put down and the call hung up.

It was a long twenty-four hours and Stewart got very little rest, but what she did do was visit the body of the man she had shot. He had been laid out in the local mortuary, heavily guarded, but they had asked if she wanted to see him. When he took back the white cloth and she saw the face of the man who had sat sedately with her on her drive from Gatwick to Inverness, Kirsten actually shed a tear. He had been a hard person not to like, for he had seemed so inoffensive, like some sort of sober businessman, a hired gun there to do a job, and he had done it well.

While she stood looking at him, she felt her hands begin to shake. Her mind flashed back to the two men on the ground beside the camper van. The three shots she had fired at the gunman had hit him every time. One had gone through his back, one had caught a shoulder, but one had hit him in the back of the head. That was why his weapon had dropped, a weapon she later found out could be taken apart and placed inside a briefcase. How he had got that briefcase, with the weapon inside, into the country, no one knew. Had he flown into Gatwick? Had he come in some other route? Nothing was known about the man until he had first spoken to Kirsten.

The roundup of the group financing the attack did not go so well. On hearing of the mission failure, Liz had clearly gone to ground, and while they were able to find the trafficked women still in the brothel house, there were few other people around. Maybe Liz had already headed away after the bodies were found near the camper van.

Kirsten wondered what she should do next, but there really was nothing to do. She would need to make a report. When she called up Anna again and only got Richard answering, she advised that she would be off for the next week, trying to treat this mental trauma she had, and that she would check in with the service doctor. She did that but found herself wandering the streets over the next couple of days. She should have been elated at what she had done. She should have been happy, preventing a murder, but instead all she saw was the face of Lars.

It probably was not his name. Identification was still going on, answers sought from across Europe, from fellow police forces and services, but no one seemed to know the man. The press was similarly quiet. An attack on the first minister was big news but it had been hushed up. Only those in the forces knew, only those who had been there. Everything was being done on the quiet until Kirsten received the phone call, advising her that she would need to come into Inverness, into the police station.

Kirsten knew it well, having worked there for nearly a year, but she still came in her casual outfit, trainers, and jacket. As she stepped out of the car, she saw a figure across the car park she knew. She put her hand up to wave, and he waved back. Macleod had been right, telling her to follow her own instincts. She went to go over to him, but a voice called advising her to come straight inside to the station. She gave an apologetic wave and saw Macleod watch her walk all the way inside. Once there, she was taken to the very top floor and found herself in a room with the Chief Constable. Six months ago, she would have been quaking at her knees to meet this person, but now he was no longer her boss; she worked for somebody else. Still, she was glad when he extended a hand and thanked her and said that someone in the next room wanted to meet her.

Kirsten did not do politics. She was never that interested in the key figures. Her life was more grounded, dealing with the troubles her brother had had and simply trying to make her wage, as first a police officer and now someone working with the services. She almost failed to clock that it was the first minister in the room with her. The woman was enthusiastic in her praise, thanking Kirsten and telling her how she would recommend her for all sorts of awards, but Kirsten refused them all saying it was just her job. The whole process lasted ninety-five minutes, and Kirsten was in no doubt that the woman was grateful, but it was definitely a politician's meeting for Kirsten reckoned that, unlike the first minister, she had spoken less than twenty words the whole time she was in.

When she exited, the chief constable seemed more interested in getting back to the first minister than saying well done again to Kirsten. On her way out of the building, she popped into the murder team office below and looked across at empty desks. She saw Ross's and the one opposite it where she used to sit. There was now someone else there. Everything on the desk was different, colourful, a scarf left over the seat. Apparently, they had got the call, had to head out as a team. Kirsten shook her head at her luck, but this was the past. It had stood her in good stead, but it was not where she was now.

Leaving the station, Kirsten drove to a residential home that she knew well, got out of the car, and knocked on the door.

The woman there smiled, buzzed the door, and let her in.

'He's in the lounge at the moment. I think he's doing a jigsaw.' Kirsten nodded, made her way along the corridor and found her brother sitting quite peacefully in front of a jigsaw of a waterfall.

When she came in, he looked up but showed no recognition. He gave a smile, but that was her brother. He smiled at everyone unless he thought there was something wrong with them.

'Do you like jigsaws?' he said to her. Kirsten thought of the number she had completed with him, and no, she did not like them, but he had loved them so she had sat at times for hours with him.

'Do you want to do this one with me? I think I'm a little bit stuck.'

Kirsten sat down beside her brother, began to take pieces out and show him where it fitted.

'You're quite good at this. Have you done many of these before?'

Kirsten felt the tear rolling down her eye.

'Are you okay? You seem a little sad.'

'It's just someone I used to know,' said Kirsten. 'You remind me so much of him.'

Her brother seemed confused by the comment and then buried his face back in the jigsaw. Kirsten sat for the next two hours completing the jigsaw with him, at which point he asked her name.

'It's Kirsten.'

'They say I knew someone called Kirsten once. It's some-where in my books, I've written it down. I write a lot of things down.' Kirsten wanted to say that she was his sister. She's the

210

one that was there, but anytime they had done it in the past, he just exploded in rage, unable to take this understanding onboard.

'I hope she was good to you,' said Kirsten.

'What about you?' he said, 'Do you have anybody special?'

'One person. He doesn't even know I exist.'

'That's hard. You must have somebody else.'

'I have friends. One of them is very old compared to us, and the other ones I just don't see a lot anymore.'

'Why's that?'

'I just work somewhere different. Life's changed a lot lately. Got to get on with it.'

When Kirsten left the home, she sat in the car and cried, but then all of a sudden, she raised her head. This had to be the start. This had to be the change. She could either be weighed down by everything that had gone wrong, or she could stand up against it. 'We're there to protect,' Macleod had said, and she would, probably in a very different way to what he did.

First up, Kirsten, I'm going home and I'm having a shower. Then, I'm going to the gym and I'm going to beat the living daylights out of someone. Then, I'm going to have another shower. When I smell fresh and good, I'm going to put on something nice, and I'm going to see if I can't meet me someone nice.

With that, she turned the keys in the ignition, flipped on the radio, and began to sing to the tune that was playing away as she turned out of the nursing home. She wondered if 'Don't Fear the Reaper' was really the correct anthem for her.

Read on to discover the Patrick Smythe series!

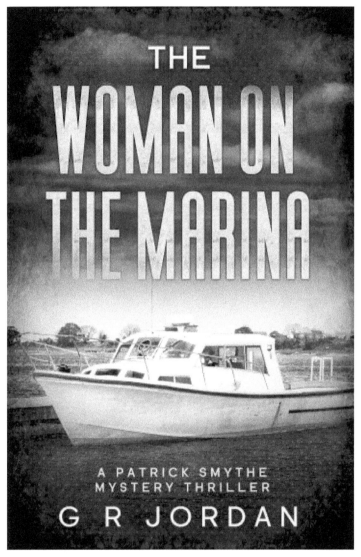

Start your Patrick Smythe journey here!

Patrick Smythe is a former Northern Irish policeman who

after suffering an amputation after a bomb blast, takes to the sea between the west coast of Scotland and his homeland to ply his trade as a private investigator. Join Paddy as he tries to work to his own ethics while knowing how to bend the rules he once enforced. Working from his beloved motorboat 'Craigantlet', Paddy decides to rescue a drug mule in this short story from the pen of G R Jordan.

Join G R Jordan's monthly newsletter about forthcoming releases and special writings for his tribe of avid readers and then receive your free Patrick Smythe short story.

Go to https://bit.ly/PatrickSmythe for your Patrick Smythe journey to start!

About the Author

GR Jordan is a self-published author who finally decided at forty that in order to have an enjoyable lifestyle, his creative beast within would have to be unleashed. His books mirror that conflict in life where acts of decency contend with self-promotion, goodness stares in horror at evil, and kindness blindsides us when we at our worst. Corrupting our world with his parade of wondrous and horrific characters, he highlights everyday tensions with fresh eyes whilst taking his methodical, intelligent mainstays on a roller-coaster ride of dilemmas, all the while suffering the banter of their provocative sidekicks.

A graduate of Loughborough University where he masqueraded as a chemical engineer but ultimately played American football, Gary had worked at changing the shape of cereal flakes and pulled a pallet truck for a living. Watching vegetables freeze at -40'C was another career highlight and he was also one of the Scottish Highlands "blind" air traffic controllers.

These days he has graduated to answering a telephone to people in trouble before telephoning other people to sort it out.

Having flirted with most places in the UK, he is now based in the Isle of Lewis in Scotland where his free time is spent between raising a young family with his wife, writing, figuring out how to work a loom and caring for a small flock of chickens. Luckily, his writing is influenced by his varied work and life experience as the chickens have not been the poetical inspiration he had hoped for!

You can connect with me on:

🌐 https://grjordan.com

f https://facebook.com/carpetlessleprechaun

Subscribe to my newsletter:

✉ https://bit.ly/PatrickSmythe

Also by G R Jordan

G R Jordan writes across multiple genres including crime, dark and action adventure fantasy, feel good fantasy, mystery thriller and horror fantasy. Below is a selection of his work. Whilst all books are available across online stores, signed copies are available at his personal shop.

The Hunted Child (Kirsten Stewart Thrillers #2)

https://grjordan.com/product/the-hunted-child

A twelve-year-old witness to a drug killing goes on the run. The murderer puts a price on the child's head. Can Kirsten Stewart pick up the girl's trail, or will she meet a bloody end from the pursuing bounty hunters?

When a young girl inadvertently stumbles upon a drug gang execution, she sets in motion a brutal hunt like the Highlands has never seen. From farmland to coast, mountain to valley, no hiding place will bring a safe haven. But when Service operative Kirsten Stewart picks up the trail, she realises there's more than one hand in play.

In her second solo novel, Kirsten has to rely heavily on her own instincts as she finds the shadowy world she now operates in becoming darker still. With the pressure of a child's life in the balance, Kirsten has to draw on all her mental and physical resources, if she is to stop an innocent girl falling to a killer's knife.

The bloody scramble for the innocent has begun…

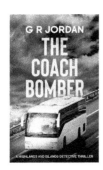

The Coach Bomber (Highlands & Islands Detective Book 14)
https://grjordan.com/product/the-coach-bomber
An airport coach blown apart. A full passenger load gives a vast list of suspects. With mounting media pressure to name a killer, can Macleod dig deep into a gang war to find a deadly hitman?

When an airport bus is blown apart on the main road out of Inverness, DI Macleod finds a press backlash when they name their own suspect. With the undercurrent of an ongoing drug war upping the ante, Macleod must rely on his Sergeant Hope McGrath to infiltrate the organisations and help bring the real killer to the light.

Don't miss your stop on the way to boomtown!

Corpse Reviver (A Contessa Munroe Mystery #1)

https://grjordan.com/product/corspe-reviver

A widowed Contessa flees to the northern waters in search of adventure. An entrepreneur dies on an ice pack excursion. But when the victim starts moonlighting from his locked cabin, can the Contessa uncover the true mystery of his death?

Catriona Cullodena Munroe, widow of the late Count de Los Palermo, has fled the family home, avoiding the scramble for title and land. As she searches for the life she always wanted, the Contessa, in the company of the autistic and rejected Tiff, must solve the mystery of a man who just won't let his business go.

Corpse Reviver is the first murder mystery involving the formidable and sometimes downright rude lady of leisure and her straight talking niece. Bonded by blood, and thrown together by fate, join this pair of thrill seekers as they realise that flirting with danger brings a price to pay.

Highlands and Islands Detective Thriller Series

https://grjordan.com/
product/waters-edge

Join stalwart DI Macleod and his burgeoning new DC McGrath as they look into the darker side of the stunningly scenic and wilder parts of the north of Scotland. From the Black Isle to Lewis, from Mull to Harris and across to the small Isles, the Uists and Barra, this mismatched pairing follow murders, thieves and vengeful victims in an effort to restore tranquillity to the remoter parts of the land.

Be part of this tale of a surprise partnership amidst the foulest deeds and darkest souls who stalk this peaceful and most beautiful of lands, and you'll never see the Highlands the same way again

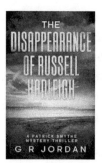

The Disappearance of Russell Hadleigh (Patrick Smythe Book 1)

https://grjordan.com/product/the-disappearance-of-russell-hadleigh

A retired judge fails to meet his golf partner. His wife calls for help while running a fantasy play ring. When Russians start co-opting into a fairly-traded clothing brand, can Paddy untangle the strands before the bodies start littering the golf course?

In his first full novel, Patrick Smythe, the single-armed former policeman, must infiltrate the golfing social scene to discover the fate of his client's husband. Assisted by a young starlet of the greens, Paddy tries to understand just who bears a grudge and who likes to play in the rough, culminating in a high stakes showdown where lives are hanging by the reaction of a moment. If you love pacey action, suspicious motives and devious characters, then Paddy Smythe operates amongst your kind of people.

Love is a matter of taste but money always demands more of its suitor.

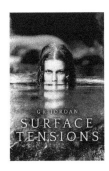

Surface Tensions (Island Adventures Book 1)
https://grjordan.com/product/surface-tensions

Mermaids sighted near a Scottish island. A town exploding in anger and distrust. And Donald's got to get the sexiest fish in town, back in the water.

"Surface Tensions" is the first story in a series of Island adventures from the pen of G R Jordan. If you love comic moments, cosy adventures and light fantasy action, then you'll love these tales with a twist. Get the book that amazon readers said, "perfectly captures life in the Scottish Hebrides" and that explores "human nature at its best and worst".

Something's stirring the water!